THE 13
TALES OF ILLUSORY

STEPHANIE AYERS

For information contact:
Stephanie Ayers
860 Rodgers Drive
Springfield, OH 45503
https://stephanieayersauthor.com

TABLE OF CONTENTS

DEDICATION

To Anastacia Campbell,
without whom I never would have
found my voice

SOUL SURVIVOR

Wandering the woods late at night
I have no candle or flashlight;
Only memory to guide my way
To the house on Devil's Cay
Where legends say an evil dwells
And rises when the ocean swells;
I never know what next I'll see
As the Devil roams the frothing sea;
Ghostly specters of ships once sailed,
The Devil they met, in a storm they
failed;
They fought with valor, their souls brave
Their strength unmatched in the Devil's
rage,
Down, down in the depths they fell
Bodies in the dark of a liquid hell.

The Devil slices through them without a
knife
Only teeth that tear the flesh with strife;
Severed heads and severed limbs
Severed dreams and severed whims,
Gathered in the bowels of their serous
grave
Prisoners held captive in a watery cave;
Each abandoned part is given new life
And the Devil takes himself a wife;

Together they rule the dark abyss
Love inhuman in its bliss;
The sea still churns strong and wild,
Their wish in creating a Devil child
Down, down in the depths still they fell
Bodies in the dark of a liquid hell.

Still I wander the woods at night
Without the moon's gentle light;
Only memory to guide my way,
To the house on Devil's Cay
Where once upon a time before
My lover sailed from its gritty shore;
To him I've given my limbs and life
To appease the Devil's wicked wife;
My soul will haunt this place no more
When his ship is once more on that
shore;
With lifeless eyes I wait and see
My lover will be returned to me.

©2012 Stephanie Ayers

IF YOU DARE

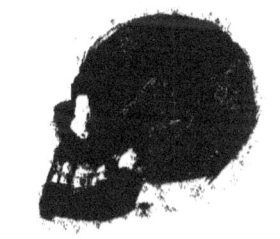

THE PUPPET MASTER

"Those puppets are going to break your heart," Finn said to Abigail as he cleaned them and tightened the screws of their joints. Abigail, absorbed in counting their profits, ignored him. "You can't take a tiger that wild and turn it to wood."

"Hmmm?" She did not look up from the bills spread out before her. Neat stacks of currency lined the small wooden table according to value.

"Nothing." He shook his head. Everything he said was important, but she only listened when she wanted to.

"You said something about turning something wild into paper…" She turned her head slightly. They shared a small circus car. It consisted of two tables, a dresser, and a bed. A nudge of her elbow would send him sprawling to the floor.

"No, I said wood. I was just musing." He laid the last puppet into the wooden box where they slept between shows. So far, every show had been successful. No one in the world had puppets as life-like as theirs. People turned out by the dozens to see them. Despite their popularity, Finn grew restless. He never had liked staying in one place too long.

"Well, stop. You aren't making any sense. Besides, I need a massage. You know how badly my neck hurts after a show. Stop playing with the puppets and give me a massage!" She packed the money tightly in an envelope and closed the safe.

She always demanded, never asked, and he always obliged. He did so now, begrudgingly. The circus tiger remained on his mind. So very wild it was, and Abigail wanted to put its likeness on paper and use it as a background for a show. The whole circus scheme, hiring them for their unusual puppet show, made him uncomfortable. He stopped massaging, running his hand through her long mahogany hair. "So, did we do it? Do we have enough?"

She turned on her stool, one smooth leg crossing and uncrossing until she faced him. Finn was a handsome man with his clean cut golden brown hair, lean shape, and dimpled smile. "No, not tonight, but it was close."

He slammed his fist on the table. "Dammit, Abby!" His eyes wandered over to the puppet box; he moved to it swiftly and pulled out two puppets. They were new, a green genie and the red-faced butcher. "And yet, you buy more puppets!"

Spittle landed on Abigail's face. She flicked it off with the back of her hand. "Yes! New puppets that will make us even more money, Finn."

Finn shook the puppets, squeezing the butcher hard enough to break him. The crack of the wood appeased him even as splinters slid into the soft pad of his palm. "Wonderful. Just what we needed!" Sarcasm dripped from his lips. "Tell me, Abigail, exactly how did you plan to fit a genie and a fat old butcher into the show? Were you going to wish for a pig?"

Abigail shrunk back, away from the fist she expected to plow into her body at any moment. Anger always got the better of Finn. It would not be the first time he'd left a bruise on her. She had decided long ago the next time he wanted to move on, she would let him. This circus was all she needed.

"Yes, we will grant the audience three wishes! What a great idea!" She shook as her hands clasped together with excitement she did not feel. "You'll see! The money will come rolling in! Then we can leave. We'll go wherever you want!"

Finn cooled down. She knew how to defuse his anger, though it did not always work. "Three wishes, eh? So how do we go about making the wishes come true unless we know about them beforehand?"

Silence pierced the tension in the room. Abigail knew exactly how to get the three wishes fulfilled. Her grandmother taught her the Romani magic well. Finn never knew where the puppets came from, never questioned until now.

Finn set about fixing the broken puppet, something he always did when he needed to think.

"I have an idea, Finn," Abigail

interrupted, a little too much glee in her voice. Luckily, Finn ignored her long enough to lay the butcher down delicately.

"What is that, Abby?" His eyes rolled sideways to look at her.

"We could set up three of our people in the audience, each holding a slip of paper with the wish we want them to share. Then, we write the story to follow and make them come true."

Finn's jaw dropped open. It was a clever idea, one that would suit all purposes. Abigail kept her face void of emotion as she waited for his response. He started to speak, stopped, examined the puppet again, tightened a screw, and stopped, then repeated the whole process once more before answering.

"I like it. Can we trust three people to play along?"

"Yes. I know three who would be willing." Abigail smiled. She knew exactly who would play along and why.

"Excellent. I'll start writing the script for tomorrow then." Finn turned to the map of the world stretched across the wall behind him.

Abigail knew he searched for where he wanted to go. She would make sure he got there. "Did you decide where we are going next?"

"Hmmm. I want to go somewhere exotic, but our funds, even if this is successful, won't allow for that. We need to move from here, though. I don't like being in one place too long, you know that. What do you think of Niagara Falls?"

She smiled again. "Sounds like a plan!"

Abigail peeked over the top of the stage. As expected, today brought a bigger audience than ever before. She knew the tiger background would be a hit. She spied her three minions and, when they returned her look, shot them the evil eye. They shivered to her satisfaction. Finn finished the opening lines, stepped behind the screen, and Abigail dropped the genie onto the stage.

"Who dares summon me from my sleep?" the genie said.

"It is I, the lonely butcher!" Finn said as Abigail dropped the puppet to the stage.

The genie's large green eyes rolled in extreme exaggeration. "Humph. Fine. I grant you three wishes. What shall they be?" Glitter sprinkled onto the stage.

"Who among you knows my plight?" The butcher pointed to the audience.

A female voice shouted from the crowd, "He wishes for his own space!"

"So shall it be!" the genie answered. She waved her wand and glitter filled the stage. A puppet sized box appeared in front of her. "Your wish is granted. You have your own space. Now, on with your second wish, or I'll feed you to the tiger!"

Another female voice, older this time, trembled, "He wishes to be thin and handsome!"

The genie waved her wand again and glitter fell over the butcher. When it cleared, a leaner, younger butcher resembling Finn stood where the old fat one had been. The genie blew a wolf whistle. "Hello, thin and handsome! Starve the tiger, and tell me your third wish?"

A male voice boomed from the audience, "I wish I was in Niagara Falls!"

Another wave of glitter filled the stage, and the butcher lay in the open box. The genie closed the box, stuck a stamp on it, and whistled for the mailman. "Wish granted."

Abigail looked at the space where Finn had stood during the show, then smiled at the new puppet in the box. "If I loved you, that's my fault. Now it's time to let you go. So long, my dearest Finn."

NO RETURNS

Amber's excitement mounted as she stepped onto her porch. A plain brown box sealed with silver duct tape sat in front of her door. She hadn't expected anything, but she picked it up and shook it. Thunk, thunk, clunk. The contents shifted and she almost dropped it. She checked the labels as she carried the box inside. The sloppy handwritten return address bore a stark contrast to the delicate print of her name. She didn't recognize the names or the writing, but her desire to open the box won over any reservations she held. She squinted at the miniscule print underneath her zip code, trying to read it.

No Returns.

Curious, she pulled at the tape until the top flaps opened and displayed the peanuts inside. Something black lurked within the white Styrofoam, like spilled charcoal in a field of snow. She sat down on the shiny wood floor and pulled a vintage camera out. It reminded her of the kind her mother took pictures with back in the '70s when she was a child. A small tag dangled from it. Written in the same careful print as her address, Amber read:

Capture a Soul

Intrigued with the camera, Amber twisted the lens cover off, not noticing the way it glared from its nakedness. A tiny label on the back of the camera repeated the words No Returns. She ignored it and opened the back, delighted to find a roll of film within. She carefully removed the roll, pleased to find it unblemished by the light.

A twisted face screamed from the first unfurled frame. A wisp of white smoke ascended from the film, caressed her skin, tickled her neck, and rot invaded her nostrils. She gasped for air, but her lungs refused to cooperate. Her lips opened in a silent scream. Splinters from the hardwood floor embedded under her nails as she choked, and her eyes bulged. The mist expelled from her mouth and zapped into the sudden flash of the camera.

A simple brown box sat outside his doorstep. Michael picked it up in excitement, wondering if his grandmother's present had finally arrived.

WADE, HAUNTED

"This isn't what I imagined heaven would look like."

Stark white light burned Wade's eyes.

"That's because it's not heaven, and you aren't dead." A pleasant faced man sat in a chair next to Wade's bed. A silver badge on his police uniform read: S. Puckett.

"Where am I?" Wade asked.

"You're in the hospital."

Wade groaned. He wanted to sit up, but the tubes attached to his body wouldn't let him. He pushed the oxygen mask away. His neatly wrapped wrists throbbed. A gasp slipped from his lips, and his eyes opened wide in surprise. "Why?"

Puckett's eyebrows stitched together and his jaw lengthened. He pulled his cellphone out, redirected the camera, and held it in front of Wade's face. Wade gasped. He tried to touch the swath of white gauze that covered his dark curls, but the pinch of his IV stopped him. A week's worth of stubble marred his jawline.

Bruised blue eyes looked back at him over a broken nose.

Puckett lowered the mirror. "Do you remember anything?"

Concrete. Water. Free falling. Steel. His short life flicking like an old movie through his head.

"N-no." Wade lied. The pain intensified as his body awoke, and he winced. "What... happened to me?"

"You slit your wrists and jumped off a bridge." Puckett set the mirror down and picked up a faded photo album. "You landed on the stern of a moving boat. We found this on you." He tipped the album forward against Wade's stomach and opened the cover. "Who are these people?"

Blood stained the edge of the album. Wade moved past it to the contents on the page. As the sultry blonde's picture came into focus, Wade's memories and arousal surfaced...

"Just one hour?"

Three heads bobbed in agreement. Wade looked at the old farmhouse and shivered. An hour until sunset. If he wanted in the fraternity, he had to do this.

"One hour. Inside. We'll be watching." Donnie tapped his watch, then elbowed the guy standing next to him.

In unison, they lined up against Donnie's BMW.

"Starting now."

The front door of the white house opened with a squeak that made Wade's heart skip a beat. His eyes closed, and the dusty silence of the long empty house accosted him. Nothing disturbed the air, not even the buzz of appliances. Sensing the vacancy, he opened his eyes. A photo album sat on the rickety coffee table just beyond the front door. His stomach clenched. Hesitant eyes searched the room as he moved towards the table, noting the crumbling paint on the walls and broken bricks of the fireplace, but he switched direction at the last minute. Despite the dead silence, he needed to know there was no one there. His feet carried him through a small opening and into the kitchen.

Cobwebs crowded dark corners, and a spider web covered the base of the sink. The stale odor of disuse exuded from the refrigerator as he opened it. Nothing there but more cobwebs. He coughed and closed it. A glance out the window showed him a yard filled with unruly weeds and tall, browning grass. He followed a short hall to a closed door. Inside the closet a few musty jackets hung on metal hangers and dust coated the floor.

A short staircase with an ornate brass bannister loomed opposite the closet. He ascended, the ominous creaking and sighing of the steps disturbing the silence. Wade's heart plunged to his belly. He raced to the top looking over his shoulder every other step. Once he reached the top, an open foyer looked down into the front room. With bated breath he investigated the rooms behind him and found most of them empty. He flipped the light switch in the bathroom out of habit, and a pasty white face stared at him from the mirror. Startled, he jumped and his heart quickened, until he realized it was his reflection.

Wade's fingers trembled as he turned the knob of the last room, and the door opened without noise. Rose pink covered the walls, and gold-framed landscapes of mountains and sunsets hung on either side of an elaborate oak dresser. A large gold headboard disappeared behind a yellowed rosebud coverlet. A layer of age and abandonment coated everything. He shut the door, a sense of intrusion replacing his dread, and moved to the railing. The album winked up at him from the coffee table, drawing his attention. His curiosity aroused, he worked his way to the front room.

A cloud of dust exhaled from the couch as he sat. His hands quivered as he opened the cover; he took his time pouring over each page. Pictures of a handsome family rose from the pages. A sincere-faced father draped an arm across each son's shoulders. A beautiful woman stood beside him, cradling an infant in her arms. As their story unfolded, the family appeared less and less, until only pictures of the woman remained. Loneliness seeped from her eyes, and he wondered what had happened to them.

With his eyes in a half-squint, he concentrated on the surrounding room, searching for a clue. A dark stain on the wall near the baseboard caught his attention. Hot breath blew against his neck. He turned and startled. The woman from the pictures sat next to him. Her ruby lips pouted coyly. Her blonde hair twisted seductively down her body, drawing attention to her full breasts. They pressed against her tight top as she leaned forward, teasing Wade with her closeness.

"What brings you here, lover?" Her sultry voice filled his ears. She kissed his cheek and stroked his chin with shiny, cherry red fingertips. The album went out of focus as Wade's heart accelerated. His mind and soul screamed to race for the BMW, but his body betrayed him, and he breathed in her perfume. Heat climbed from his cheeks to his ears. She laughed, a pleasant sound. "Oh my."

She popped a button on her blouse, releasing the pressure to her breasts. Her hand brushed across his thighs. "Is this why you've come? To please a lonely woman?" She stretched her leg out, knocking the album from his lap. A bare foot dropped between his legs, stroking, and everything else fled from his mind. She pressed her lips against his as she straddled him, grinding her hips and thrusting her bosom against his chin. His eyes closed, and a moan escaped his throat. She wrapped her lips around his earlobe and breathed into his ear.

"You're mine."

When he opened his eyes, she had disappeared.

A horn blared outside and Wade jumped. He survived the hour. He pulled his shirt up to swipe the sweat from his brow. A soft whiff of her perfume lingered on his shirt. A small wet spot on his pants made him question his sanity. She wasn't real, was she? Embarrassment overwhelmed him as he thought about what his friends would say if they knew. He pulled his pants a little higher on his waist so his shirt covered the spot.

As he rose from the couch, the album fell open to the last page. The woman lay in a casket, a shriveled shell of herself. He could hear her laughing at him, mocking him. Wade froze. His heart slammed against his chest, and he choked on his breath. Was it nothing but a joke? Did the guys plan this? Had he been Punk'd? He centered his breathing as he waited for someone to jump out from behind the wall, snickering.

His lips still tasted her kiss. His lap tingled, remembering her warmth. Tendrils of fear crept up his spine. Everything in the past hour had happened. It was not a trick his friends concocted. Her laughter filled the room, breaking his thoughts. The hair on the back of his neck rose. At that moment, he remembered her last words. She had claimed him, and he now belonged to her. He needed to get out of there. He tucked the album under his arm and left the house.

"What's that?" Donnie pointed to the album.

Wade didn't answer at first. They'd think him foolish, and he wasn't ready to admit what had happened to him in the house. "Nothing, man. Let's go."

Another guy thumped Wade on the back. "Dude, you look like you saw a ghost!" he said. "Welcome to Alpha Delta! I knew you could do it!"

Wade offered a fake smile. This was what he had wanted, but now, his experience dampened his enthusiasm. He felt violated, as if he'd already lost his soul. He couldn't shake the memory of the soft, supple female he'd held in his arms. Anger replaced the fear. "Let's just go."

A week later the album spread open on his lap as he sat down on his bed. His finger traced the face of the woman within it. His eyes closed and his lips pursed expectantly but nothing happened. Wade's body craved her touch, her smell. He didn't know how he would get through the day of classes. He had to see her again. If she wouldn't come to him, he'd figure out a way to get to her.

"Come," she cooed from the album.

When he opened his eyes, Donnie stood in front of him, eyeing the album. Wade closed it hastily, cleared his throat, and set it on the bed. He pushed Donnie ahead of him. He hesitated in the doorway, his eyes seeking the album and finding it. His heart crescendoed in his chest. "No," he murmured. "I have to go to class. Later, I promise."

Donnie heard Wade mumble. "Are you talking to me?"

"No." Wade shook his head.

Donnie always waited for him, but this was the first time he'd come into the room. Donnie's eyes followed Wade's and rested on the album. He put a hand on Wade's shoulder. "You've been weird since that house, man. You sure nothing happened there?"

Pink flesh flashed in Wade's head and scorched his lips with memory. He muttered and pushed past Donnie.

"I'm serious. We need you on the morning b-ball court, man. We're getting obliterated without you." Donnie tapped the books tucked into Wade's elbow. "Can't wait 'til Finals are over to get you back."

Wade looked at an imaginary watch on his wrist. "Let's go. We'll be late for class."

He turned back to his room, his eyes catching sight of the album once more. She called to him again. He shifted the wont between his legs, shut the door, and went to class.

Wade couldn't concentrate on anything. Sweet oriental musk filled his senses. Goosebumps crawled up his arms with invisible caresses. He couldn't get her out of his head. Her voice dripped from every page; every spoken word, her lips suckling his ear. She wouldn't leave him alone. A pencil snapped in his grip, drawing all eyes to him.

"Is there a problem, lover?" The professor snapped from her seat, rattling him. "I said, is there a problem, Mr. Welch?"

Wade shrank into his desk, his cheeks scorched. "May I be excused?"

"That's up to you. It's not my student loans that have to be repaid if you fail."

Wade's face burned with fire. As he flew from the room a familiar snicker followed him. The hallway stood empty. No one could help him. He had to shut her up once and for all.

"I just wanted her to leave me alone. It's either be with her or be stuck thinking of her forever." Wade wailed.

"Did it work?"

On cue, her voice filled the hospital room, drawing Wade's attention to the holster on Puckett's hip. "Look, there!"

"No." Wade ripped the IV from his arm, tore the wires from his chest, and rose from the bed, Puckett's gun locked within his sight.

SEASON OF CHANGE

Day 6

I never did care for neighbors; always wantin' to burrah a cuppa sugar, or an egg, your hammer, or conversate. The old neighbors were a sight better than the new ones, though they've ne'er burrahed a thing from me. The old neighbors took care of their yard, always plantin grass seeds, trimmin' them hedges, weedin' and plantin', plantin' and weedin'. In fact, it was odd if'n you didn't see at least one of them with their pants soiled about the knees from dirt. Ayup. It was even more suspicious when they jus' up and sold the house jus' before the frost came 'round last winter.

I knew the new neighbors would be trouble from the git go. It was jus' somethin' 'bout the way they drove up in that flashy red pickup, what with all them bells and whistles, lookin' as though it ne'er seen dirt, jus' all purty and shiny like, the wheels all silvery and flashin' in the sun. Just plain blindin' if'n you asked me. Ain't no sense to be showin' off like that in a li'l ol' place like this. Jus' ain't no sense to it a'tall.

So, winter turned to spring, spring to summer, and I'll be damned if it ain't fall again. Fall means leaves, and leaves I jus' cain't do. This is the sixth day in a row I been out rakin' up these leaves. Though. I ain't seen hide nor hair of them out rakin' their leaves. They jus' sittin' all over their lawn, red splotches on gold flecks, on more red. Red like blood. I've already done gone and raked up their leaves what keep blowin' over in my yard. Cain't seem to keep 'em out. I'lls just hafta put a note on their door ask'n 'em to keep up with their leaves. T'ain't nothin' else what I could do.

Day 9

Damn neighbors. I know they saw it. I know it. And me, out here wipin' the sweat off'n my brow, rakin' these leaves, lookin' at their yard full of 'em. Watchin' the wind blow 'em right back into my yard where I jus' raked. The way the wind dances with 'em jus' sets my blood to boilin'. It's obscene is what it is. There's jus' no accountin' for it. None a'tall.

Day 17

Damn neighbors, cain't follow the simplest instructions. Damn leaves. Blood red. Leaves. Ever'where.

Day 22

Damn neighbors. Damn leaves. Damn red leaves. Blood. Boilin'. Leaves like blood ever'where. Boilin' blood.

Day 30

Damn leaves. Cain't see the grass for the leaves anymore. Nothin' but red, ever'where. Red like blood. Damn neighbors. Damn red.

Smash.

Damn blood. Damn tree.

Day 45

Chop. Chop. Slam. Timber! Ha. That'll take care of your damn leaf problem and your damn red truck, too. Ayup. Let's see the wind dance with your leaves now. Damn tree. Let's see you clean them leaves up now, damn neighbors. Damn blood.

Boilin' red.

Day 60

Smash. Damn neighbors.

Squish. Oh now you git that fear in your eyes? I ask'd you nicely to Rake. *Smack.* Your. *Smash.* Damn. *Rip.* Leaves.

Slash. I even wrote it up all nice an' neat on that purty stationary my wife used to use. She shore did like that red paper. Boilin' red.

Splunk. T'weren't a difficult request. All's you needed was a rake.

Squarsh. Now look it what you made me go 'n do!

Slam. All's ya had to do was ask to burrah the damn rake. *Scratch.* Look it that. Blood on your floor. Red as them leaves. Don'tcha wish you'd a listened to the nice friendly note now?

Scratch.

Scritch. Damn. Now I gotta rake 'em up for ya.

Creak. I'm gonna burrah your freezer, okay?

Slide. Oof. Thud.

Slide. Thunk. Oosh. Thud. Slap. Don't worry. *Slam.*

Your yard'll be jus' fine. Once them leaves are gone, and the frost done moved on, your flowers will be pushin' right on up through the ground in no time. No time a'tall. All's you need is a spade. Ayup. All's you need is a spade.

The 13

ON THE NINTH DAY

Four sets of eyes stared at Cassidy through her curtains. They hovered there, in the shade of the tall trees that surrounded her domain. Ever since she found the severed head of Mimir, the last of Odin's magical artifacts, and unlocked Odin's 18th song, they'd been there—two ravens and two wolves. The severed head's prediction of death scared her enough, but now the animals visited her dreams as well and kept her awake at night.

The only benefit she'd had from collecting Odin's things was the ninth day appearance of a new ring. Each new ring increased in value, gaining her the reputation of owning the finest rings in the world. Even her own ring, Odin's original gold band, found in a chest at the bottom of the sea, held high enough value that if she sold it, the money from the sale would provide for the rest of her life. She admired the ring once more, twisting it on her finger as she felt the glare of the wolves on her again.

The small chime hanging over the front door of her shop jingled, signaling the arrival of a customer. She shrugged off her lack of sleep from the dreams and planted a smile on her face.

"Hello, Max," she purred, recognizing the tan fedora and long coat of the customer. "What brings you here today?"

At the sound of his name, he turned, a scowl on his face, dark circles under his eyes. "I wish to make a return," he said.

Crap, she thought, managing to keep the smile planted on her face. She pointed to a sign in front of her cash register. **No Returns** was etched in black on a white placard attached to the register by a magnet.

"I'm so sorry, Max. What's wrong with it?"

Max slammed the ring down on the counter. The brilliant blue sapphire flashed in the light. "It's cursed," was his simple reply.

Fear iced her heart. "Cursed?"

"Yes! Myra said yes, then no,

and told me to return it. It's worthless to me."

"Even if I did take returns, Max, buyer's remorse wouldn't be a good enough reason to take it back. I'm sorry she turned you down. Perhaps you should let her keep it."

He lifted his hat and raked his fingers through his jet-black hair. "She doesn't want it. She said there's something wrong with the ring. Please, Cassidy, I beg you, take it back." His large hands cupped hers. She looked into his eyes.

"I'm sorry, Max, but I can't. If I took back every broken heart, I'd be out of business. I just can't do it." She turned the ring over in her hand, admiring its brilliance, and handed it back. Her voice softened, though her heart remained cold. "Good luck."

Howling followed Max's departure. Cassidy ran to the window expecting trouble and only found the wolves, their noses lifted and mouths parted. Sweat beaded her forehead, and she shivered as she flipped the sign to "closed" and bolted the front door. A glance at her calendar marked eight days since she'd sold the ring to Max; eight days since she'd unlocked Odin's 18th song.

She opened her safe and pulled out the parchment hidden within it. She unfolded it and caressed the exposed runes. Her fingers grazed over the ancient markings, allowing the engraved chaos of their disorderliness to cloud her mind. She needed them to make sense. She had to read them in the right order or it wouldn't work. Repeatedly the runes tumbled through her mind, weaving and tangling until they became one.

IS-TYR HAGAL-AR RIT OS-LAF FA-UR-THORN-EH KA-MAN-YR NOD-BAR GIBOR-SIG IS-TYR HAGAL-AR RIT OS-LAF FA-UR-THORN-EH KA-MAN-YR NOD-BAR GIBOR-SI

Over and over she chanted: True ego to sacrifice; Universe to ascend; Ceremonial; To accept cosmic law; To help, to heal, to project cosmic union; Capability, spirituality, roots; Karma to descend; Life, self to win. *IS-TYR HAGAL-AR RIT OS-LAF FA-UR-THORN-EH KA-MAN-YR NOD-BAR GIBOR-SIG* rose louder, and a ghostly wind whipped through her hair. The severed head's deep voice muttered behind her, "Beware! Beware!"

The sky beyond her window darkened as dark grey clouds rolled in. The wolves howled louder as the ravens cawed and beat their wings on the window panes. She heard the cacophony of eight hooves overhead.

The house shook from a powerful voice. "Who has called me from the depths of Hel? Who dares to rouse the great Odin from his sleep?" Odin descended from her ceiling, his trusty spear aimed for her throat. "What damned soul braves the secret of the 18th song?"

Cassidy gathered her courage and stood tall, facing him. "Nine times has the ring reproduced, each time joining two. Eighteen souls in my possession, now I possess YOU!"

Odin roared as his essence merged into her body. She rocked, convulsing to the floor. Her eyes closed and a smile of satisfaction formed on her face.

The bright light of the sun woke Cassidy. Two wolf silhouettes cast long shadows across her bedroom floor. The ravens spoke to her from the window.

"Good morning, sire. We've missed you."

"Good morning, Huginn, Muninn. Has it been that long? To me, Geri and Freki, to me!" The wolves turned and faced Cassidy, their tails wagging gently. They moved slowly towards her outstretched hand. She petted them thoughtfully. "Come, my loves, we have work to do. Nine rings I need returned to me, then we will Hunt and the earth will be ours again."

Eight doors she knocked on, requesting the rings back. Eight times, blood bathed her spear. Only one ring remained to complete the cycle. Max was next. No one answered the door. She knocked on the door again with the tip of her spear, still no one answered. A neighbor tending his lawn nearby spoke up, waving.

"Good morning, Cassidy! I'm afraid you just missed Myra."

"I'm looking for Max," she said.

"Max is gone. He threw this ring across the yard, packed a bag, and left. I haven't seen him since." He eyed the spear nervously and held the ring up.

She grabbed his wrist and thrust the spear in his side. She watched as shock weaved across his face. "Yes, thank you, sir. This is exactly what I was looking for." As the neighbor fell lifeless to the ground, his blood staining the azaleas, she tossed two coins on his body. "For safe passage, my friend. May your journey be peaceful."

Cassidy noted the pink tinges creeping into the horizon. Muninn landed on her shoulder. Freki joined her side. "Soon, Muninn, soon." They returned to her house.

The old grandfather clock struck midnight, ending the eighth day. The wolves' howl shook the very foundation of the house. Cassidy sat up in bed, as a great horse crashed through her window. A sinking feeling welled up in the pit of her stomach. The gold ring that started them all burned the flesh of her finger. On the bedside table, she saw a new ring, a gorgeous sparkle of three interlaced triangles. She knew she would never touch it.

Pain erupted between her thighs and continued up her body, as if someone sliced her in half with a knife. She screamed until the pain silenced her. It was not until the last of the pain slid through her brain she knew no more.

Odin rose up. "It's a pity." He put his signature ring on his finger, "All her power and she didn't recognize the 18th for what it was—the end. Come, friends, let us raise the warriors and ride the Wild Hunt. Then, we can start this earth anew."

STRIKE A POSE

The artist stood back and considered his masterpiece with a critical eye. His rendition of the girl was so life-like, he almost expected her to stand up and walk off the canvas, but it was not finished. He looked at his model: it needed something more. He grabbed a letter opener from his desk and sliced a thin line across her neck. He spread the incision open. He stepped back, made a box with his fingers, and sized up his work. He shook his head, dissatisfied. He grabbed the dropper from the easel and dipped it in the small bucket filled with Logan's blood. A few drops on her neck offered the effect he aimed for, but still, it wasn't right. He turned one dangling arm out, slit her wrist, and applied more blood until it crested the fresh wound. He let her arm drop and studied the painting through his finger box once more. He nodded in gratification and stepped behind the canvas again, ready to finish his work.

From her airy position, Logan watched him slice her throat then do the same to her wrist. She'd been on her way to see her fiance, Jack, when the killer intercepted her. Her stomach squirmed, and bile rose to her throat. Her lips curled, and her nostrils flared. Her fists clenched and unclenched, as her heart quickened. She'd been three days shy of her 21st birthday, and knew Jack had planned something special for her.

Now she lay sprawled naked on a Louis XIV couch, her body pressed against a plush pink blanket. The killer had hidden the bruises he'd put between her thighs by applying makeup in strategic places, leaving a hint of purple for effect. She admitted he had talent, which angered her further.

Whispers erupted around the artist. Logan's back hitched, and she turned her head from side to side to find the source, until she realized they belonged to his other victims. She listened as they shushed each other.

She wanted to see them, but they remained hidden, sharing only their voices.

"He's done it again."

"This girl is his best yet."

"Too bad for the girl."

"Someone needs to stop him, poor girl."

"I'm not just some girl, my name is Logan!" Her anguished voice rose above the rest. They ignored her.

Silence. The killer had finished. He stepped back and examined his work. Perfection! He cupped his hands in front of him, sizing it up from all directions. A wicked smile slashed his face and his hands clapped with pleasure. Anyone would be lucky to own it.

"This is my greatest work yet, and I know exactly who to call." The killer picked up the phone. "I hope he's still in the market." He fingered a business card in one hand, as he pressed the keys on the phone with the other.

He meant to sell the painting?! Horror settled in Logan's throat. She swallowed.

"What kind of person buys these paintings? He must be as sick as the artist! And the audience! What kind of people..." No one responded. Perhaps they didn't have the answers, either.

A tremor shook Logan. Her blood boiled, and heat warmed her cheeks. Her belly coiled. She wanted to eliminate this artist, and if someone bought her painting she'd have to destroy him, too. As long as someone existed to buy the art, the danger remained.

"I've got a fresh painting for you. It's drying now. It will be ready for viewing in a couple of days. Do you want to see it?" He paused, and a hedonistic smile emerged. He'd been successful.

Red flashed in front of Logan's eyes. She stomped. Her nostrils flared. Her fists pummelled the empty air. This evil must be stopped, no matter the consequences. She'd find a way to use the monster receiving her painting as a pawn to capture the savage that put her in it. No one else would die to satisfy this devil's urges again.

He hung up and looked at the painting again. He dipped the paintbrush in the bucket and scribbled his signature across the bottom right corner. She hovered in front of it, hoping to catch his name, but all she saw was an "S". Despite her desire to search his studio, translucent strands kept her secured between her body and the painting.

The killer cackled. "Oh yes, this one will earn me a fortune! I could do four or five more with this girl alone!"

He stretched out his hands to form a box again and viewed the scene in front of him. He put a blank canvas on the easel and stepped back. He repositioned Logan's naked corpse, flipped her on her belly, then pushed her upwards onto her knees and spread them. Her breasts dangled, her right hip leaned against the soft back of the couch, and her butt hung in the air. He crossed her wrists over each other on the armrest, and set her head on her hands, her face turned towards him.

He dipped a paintbrush in the bucket, held it over her, and let the blood drip down. It traveled along the cut on her neck and dripped on her arms, the red a sharp contrast against her ashen skin. He looked through the finger box again and simpered, pleased with what he saw. As he stepped away, gravity pulled her to the floor, leaving a trail of blood in its wake. Scarlet-faced, he snapped a paintbrush in two. He wanted to paint.

He shoved her roughly on the couch, not caring how she landed. He raised his hand as if to smack her, but the vase of roses on the table behind the couch distracted him. He stepped back, boxing the vase with his hands, and squinted one eye. He left the room and broughta machete with his return. His eyes gleamed once before he swung the blade up over his head and into her flesh, severing her head from her neck in a single blow. He grasped her by her hair, set her head on top the vase, scattered the roses around it, and stepped back. It needed something more. He picked up the bucket and emptied it into the vase. With sadistic satisfaction, he picked up another paintbrush and whistled.

The sheer shock of her dismemberment left Logan speechless. The voices had abandoned her, frightened by the macabre captured on the canvas.

"How long must I watch?" Logan asked the silence.

A gentle voice answered. "Look around. What do you see?"

This new voice possessed a kindness that made Logan wish she had known the person behind the voice while they both still lived.

Logan's muscles tightened and resisted against the translucent threads. Her inner sight awakened. "I see nothing but carnage... blood. I see where prior murders took place and evidence that he's done similar things to other women. The dried blood on the wall tells me I'm not the first, while his anger tells me I won't be the last." Sadness overwhelmed her.

"And the paintings? Can you see those?"

Nothing marred the white landscape of the walls, though sometimes she saw bruises where something used to hang. "No. There are no paintings."

"Look harder!"

Logan let her eyes settle on the back wall. Spectres of frames containing faded paintings emerged from it. The bright colors and red gashes gave identity to the gruesomeness displayed on the blurred canvases. Four, eight, twelve, twenty, Logan counted each as they appeared, overlapping the others as they faded.

"There," the voice said, as another painting emerged, clearer than the others. The woman had been posed similar to the way she was, except for the belly that bulged with life. Nausea chased her heart, and Logan wept.

"Is that you?" she whispered. Silence. "He won't get away with this."

A gentle sigh. "How will you do that? You can't leave."

Logan looked down at the ghostly tendrils. "Look!" She pointed to her legs. "I'm attached to the painting. He's going to sell it. I'll go with it!"

"Impossible. Once the painting leaves, that connection is completely broken."

A new voice joined in. "Do you think we want to watch this over and over?"

A chorus of voices chimed in like an echo. "No—oh—oh—oh—oh!"

"But you're ghosts!" Logan said, shocked. "You can go wherever you want!"

"Not that simple," the voices said as one.

"It has to be." Discouragement laced her words.

"I have heard of a way," a soothing, comforting voice chimed in.

"Oh?" The unity of the voices disoriented Logan.

"But she is the only one who can do it." The voice paused for effect.

"You've been here the longest. Why haven't you told us before?" Another voice accused.

"No one's ever had the will to ask."

The voices silenced. A cool breeze wafted through the room. Logan waited for instructions.

"The cost is heavy," the voice warned.

"I don't care." Logan said. The lack of breath and absence of a racing heart pricked her insides. Nausea returned in her bowels.

"You must choose the painting, but it's not as easy as you think. When you leave your body behind, your soul will be trapped, unable to move on. It could be impossible to find your body, let alone connect to it, once you've severed the link. There's no hope that somehow your soul will reconnect. It won't."

"So, let me get this straight. If I do this, I'll be trapped in the painting forever?"

"Quite probably. It's a big sacrifice to make when there's no guarantee that it'll work, either. It could mean eternal separation from everyone, a death sentence to the purgatory on canvas."

Silence. Logan hesitated. She didn't know if the sacrifice was worth it. Jack's smile bobbed in front of her.

Her chest caught. Pain threatened to drown her. She would never see him again, not even in the afterlife, if she did this. Suffocating fire welled up in her chest, and she gasped.

"Do you still want to do this?" the voice interrupted. "You're the only one who can. We've been here too long."

Logan's eyes shifted to the fibers again. The one connected to her body grew thicker every second. Her window of opportunity would disappear.

"Ok." A tremor raced through her. She shook it off. "I'll do it."

"The pain you'll feel is great. I tried once. I barely survived the soul ripping. The pain and the sacrifice of never seeing my children again was too much for me." A sigh filled the emptiness left by sorrow. "No one else has tried. The lifeline to the painting weakens as the one connected to your body strengthens. It will take that much more to relinquish it. You must separate and resist the pull of your soul to your body. You can start anytime you'd like, but don't start unless you're absolutely certain."

Logan reached for the filament that tethered her to the painting. She followed it until she could grip the canvas with both hands. A sharp tug on her feet loosened her grip, but she held firm. Urgent tugs pulled at her feet and clawed her calves. Horrific tearing filled the air.

Pain stifled Logan. The agony of her rape, followed by her suffocation was nothing compared to this. Every limb in her astral body snapped. The pain seared through her like she'd been set on fire. It began at her crown, pressed down on her brain, scorched her nasal cavity, burned down her throat, scalded her insides, and shot fire through her limbs. She wanted to curl into a fetal position, but she couldn't let go of the canvas.

A new pain penetrated her defenses. A knife peeled at her essence, one layer at a time. She gasped, sucking the air in search of relief. Each new layer stripped brought greater pain. Living, she'd have passed out by this point. As a ghost, she didn't have that luxury. She wanted to explode, but there was nothing she could do except release the painting and give in to the calling of her soul. Logan sobbed.

"Oh!" she said, her pain palpable in her voice.

"There's no going back now! Pull yourself into the painting quickly!" The voices joined together, cheering her on.

She mustered her strength and planted her feet on the canvas, wincing and gasping as she forced them into the painting. The rest of her followed until only her forearms and hands remained outside, still gripping the corners. Relief flooded her as the pain lessened. She lifted one hand from the corner and pulled it in. When nothing happened, she released the other hand and, with a great sigh of relief, found herself submerged in the painting.

"Well, I did it," she said. Quiet greeted her. She was alone. Now that she'd entered the painting, there were no voices, only an empty silence. "Now what?"

She moved to the corner where the killer left his autograph. She could only see a giant "S". She kicked the dangling foot of her body double. "I should've waited. Something in that room would've given me his name!"

An idea occurred to her. "Dammit! Why didn't I think to ask if they knew his name? I'm such an idiot!" She kicked herself again.

"Quit it!" Herself said.

Startled, Logan spun around and stared at her body sprawled grotesquely on the couch. "Did you say something?"

Painted eyes blinked. "Yes. I said quit it."

"You can talk!"

"Of course I can."

"This changes everything! Can you read my thoughts, or do I have to share them?"

Interest showed in her twin's eyes. "Let's try it."

An arm rose and rested itself on the couch. She crossed her thighs. The other arm covered her breasts self-consciously.

"Amazing!"

"I know how to fix this! I can make you move." The plan finalized in Logan's mind. Her head nodded with confidence. "Sister, we got this!"

Grey shadows lingered over the painting. Logan realized this meant someone stood close by. Due to the recent thumps and bumps and new voices surrounding her, she knew the painting had changed hands. Fire burned within her. It wasn't enough that she'd been murdered, but her ordeal—her torture—had been captured forever. The world could ogle her naked body, splayed out on that couch, her blood creeping, and she could do nothing about it. She would relive this shame every day.

Perhaps this was why none of the others ever tried. If she'd remained with her body, she wouldn't be forced to experience the intrusive judgment of strangers. She wondered if the rubberneckers understood what they saw. She caught the muffled conversations in front of her painting and listened.

"Why would anyone subject themselves to being immortalized

like this? I mean, it's just such a bizarre scene," a tenor said.

"Look at the others! They are all grisly, but not quite like this." A soft, deep female countered, a hint of high society captured in her voice. "I don't understand it myself, but I can't take my eyes off it."

A third voice, genderless in timbre, floated through the painting. "It's like an accident. You can't help looking."

"Yes, that's right. That poor girl. I hope she got paid properly." The tenor spoke again.

"Bah. This is porn in the form of art created merely for the shock. Such filth. Why would anyone accept payment to pose like this?" The female spat.

"No! They don't understand at all." Logan said aloud. Dismay clouded her vision. She closed her eyes and focused on her twin. "Aha!" she murmured, spying the small blanket draped across the back of the couch. Her painted hand reached out, snagged it, and spread it over her painted body.

"Wait, Elisandra. Where is the porn?" the tenor questioned.

Hot wind rushed across the canvas. The tenor was so close Logan could almost make out his facial features.

A tap shook the canvas. "She was naked just a moment ago. What the hell?" A raspy gasp fell from Elisandra's throat. "Marcus! Marcus!" she shouted. Her heels clicked on the tile as her shadow grew faint.

"Marcus? I've heard that name before." Logan's eyes squeezed shut as she concentrated. The killer's voice filled her memory and she remembered. *The buyer!* "Good, Elisandra. This is exactly what I want you to do!" She turned to her twin, still covered with the blanket. "Now what?"

Her twin blinked but remained still. Logan waited for Elisandra to return with Marcus. She held her breath in anticipation and returned her body to its original pose.

"Marcus, look! There's a blanket covering a naked woman. It wasn't there before. How do you explain that?" Elisandra said.

Marcus's hot breath hit the canvas. When the heat went away, she made her move.

"Woman, are you mad? The only blanket I see is on the back of the couch the model is sitting on." Marcus's voice halted.

"What the...?" the tenor started. Four breaths hit the large canvas, hovering so close she could smell them. "Marcus, what's wrong with this painting?"

A finger traced over Logan's painted silhouette standing in the lower right corner of the canvas. Her eyes closed, and she angled her head to reveal the gash in her neck. When the hot breaths subsided, she stretched her painted arms out like a crucifix. The blood-caked slashes on her wrists stood out. Hot breaths hovered once more, and the collective gasps rippled through the canvas.

"Marcus! Oh my god, Marcus! This woman..." the horror-struck genderless voice said.

Logan smiled. This was easier than she thought. Just for further effect, however, she made herself regain the original pose.

"Look! She's on the couch again, just like she was in the beginning," the tenor said.

Logan rolled her painted head slowly to the opposite side. It didn't go unnoticed. "No. I'm sorry, Marcus. I have to go. This is... disturbing." The staccato of a man's oxfords on linoleum bounced from the walls and pinged against the canvas. She half-smiled in pride. She high-fived her twin and heard a gasp in response.

"Marcus, are you seeing this? Is this animation of some kind because otherwise, the alternative..." Elisandra's voice trailed off in a mixture of disbelief and warning.

Logan continued making small movements with her twin. When heated breath blasted the canvas, she knew her plan had worked.

"Er, um, uh..." Marcus' voice stumbled for words. Sweat pooled on his forehead. "The, uh, the artist is...the artist is trying something new." Logan heard the confidence building as he continued speaking. "It's his next greatest achievement."

Logan paused, shocked. *Does he know?* She gasped. Renewed resolve filled her.

"Hmm," the genderless voice said. "Why animate the model versus the blood flow? That would attract more people, but this? This is horrifying, and I've lost all interest in it." The voice paused for dramatic effect. "It's without apology that I retract my bid on this scandalous piece of art. In fact, I retract my bids on anything this artist created. I won't be giving him a recommendation. Good day."

Elisandra's voice overpowered the soft footfalls of retreat. "I agree. To be honest, this artist is morbid and inhumane. Honestly, he's quite sick. I'll take my money elsewhere!" Elisandra's heels struck the tile harshly as she stomped off.

Soft breathing filtered in from beyond the canvas. She moved a small throw pillow across the couch before her twin rose and moved to the center of the portrait. The grey shadow of his silhouette grew darker. As he watched, she reenacted the brutality she'd been subjected to and ended her drama with the scene on the couch.

The quiet tapping of fingers on a keypad bounced off the canvas. A phone rang distantly, and, after a short pause, Marcus's muffled voice spoke into it. "I need to speak to a detective. I'd like to report a murder."

A CHILD LOST

Jonas, Alfie, and Sahara knew all about the underworld. They spent most of their summers growing up beneath the surface of the duck pond. They swam together with the same efficiency as the other creatures that dwelt under the surface—the silver trout, the small orange fish they never learned the names of, and, of course, the pixies. They swam as if they were born with gills, breathing freely in the water without them, until their heads breached the surface once more. Until, like all the other children before them, they didn't return.

The pond grew dark and murky with loneliness. The pixies bobbed above the surface on full moon nights and howled their pain to the golden grains of the fields. So great was their pain, they dug trenches under the pond until they could dig no more. The farmhouse foundation blocked their way until they found a way through it, sharpening their teeth as they ate their way through.

And through.

And through.

They tumbled through the nursery wall unseen. They scampered across the carpet leaving tiny wet footprints on the beige carpet. A fat orange-striped tabby stepped between them and the cradle. A pixie easily dispatched the cat with a flash of his wrist. Blood flowed onto the carpet from the gash in the animal's neck, and a strange guttural mewing crept from its throat in response. Feet larger than they were accustomed to stomped into their midst, scattering them.

Jonas roared as he entered the nursery. He raised a broom above his head and slammed it down. The first time it hit the floor, it swept the pixies into a corner of the room. He rose the broom again, this time taking aim. Two pixies flattened onto the carpet this time. He rose the broom again and again, crimson splatters on the carpet the evidence of his wrath. Only one pixie had the courage to mount the cradle, climbing with ease until he reached the top. He opened his wings and let them flutter, taking advantage of the wind they created to make the child's eyes open. A small whimper brought Jonas to the cradle. Jonas stopped, shocked.

"Azrika!" Jonas shouted. "Why?"

"You abandoned us. You must pay for our pain!"

"Take me then. Leave the baby alone, please, I beg you."

"We had you once and now you are of no use to us. A child found for a child lost, and we will disturb you no more."

Jonas' mind eye flickered back over the years to the day he had met the pixies. His parents had just bought the farmhouse two weeks before, and he'd stumbled on the pond accidentally as he explored. During his third lap across the pond, something cold and hard wrapped around his ankle and pulled him down. He fought the force holding him under until air escaped from his lungs and filled them again. Black pupil-less eyes stared from beneath Jonas' captive foot. The translucent blue hand on his ankle connected to a body topped with a shocking white patch of hair and a wicked smirk filled with pointy teeth on its face. Flashing lights redirected his attention, and the pixie let go as he swam towards them.

"Welcome, welcome! I am Azrika, king of the pixies. We are delighted to have you here. Please, take your time!" Another pixie, a bit older in appearance, greeted Jonas as he approached. The pixie's arm swept through the water in invitation. "Go, delight yourself. We are always here, and it's always free. Show me your winnings on your way out."

Dark eyes glistened from the depths. Jonas swam to the first ride, a roller coaster that rose high above them and dipped straight back down to the bottom. He shot harpoon darts at water balloons until he won a prize. He raced through a maze of flora. He played so hard it exhausted him. It was then he noticed the light from the surface had disappeared and breathing under water had become even easier. It was time to go home.

Jonas swam for the surface, but the carnival stopped him.

"Excuse me," Jonas asked the game booth attendant. "Which way is the exit?"

The pixie pointed behind him. "The funhouse is the only way out. Go through the maze of mirrors, and it will bring you back out to the surface."

Jonas thanked him and made his way to the attraction. Azrika met him there.

"Ready to go home, now? I trust you enjoyed yourself?"

"I did. It's amazing here! I'll be back tomorrow, I promise!"

Azrika licked his lips in expectation. "Good, good. Alas, I cannot let you return."

Jonas' eyebrows raised in confusion. "What? Why not?"

"We were kind enough to let you in on our secret. If we let you go now, you'll tell other people about it. We just can't have that."

"What if I promise not to tell? Will you let me go home then?"

Azrika grinned. "Of course, but only if you bring friends back with you. And if you ever tell, your fate will be the same as theirs."

Jonas first shared it with Alfie and Sahara, who also promised never to tell. Together, the trio had led too many children to the pond, helped the pixies enchant them with the wonders of the underworld. Jonas watched as even Alfie and Sahara eventually succumbed to the darkness, choosing eternal play over keeping the secret any longer. The carnival under the water drew them all in with its childish delights. The funhouse of mirrors distorted their shapes and made them laugh until they found themselves trapped within the bubbles created from their mirth. They floated to the giant wheel where they entered as children but left as small orange fish. These were the reasons he'd turned his back on the pixies. He couldn't handle the guilt of leading his friends to the pond. He knew the secret and suffered the agony of silence.

"No. You can't have her," Jonas said, his focus returning to the present.

A wicked grin spread across the pixie's face as he pointed to the empty cradle. "She's already ours."

THE MAY QUEEN

If you walk through the woods on May 1 of any given year, and it's quiet enough, you might hear the songs and laughter as 14 little girls emerge from the field. If the light is exactly right, you might even see them dancing in their ancient white dresses, flowers adorning their hair and dresses, holding bright colored ribbons attached to a wooden pole, erected in the dead center of the field. And if you are really lucky, you just might see the wolf and the girl dancing around the maypole.

This vision could haunt you for the rest of your life, or so I've been told.

Fourteen was the number of girls chosen to dance around the maypole in 1687. It was an annual event, the celebration of Beltane, the emergence of spring. It was one that the small township loathed to miss. The year before the number had been low, the May Queen barren, and as a result the crops rotted, the livestock was infected, and the town fared poorly all around.

The maypole dance was not for the squeamish. Most were reluctant to dedicate their daughters to the task, though all were expected to do it anyway. The girls usually came away tainted by something. We'd never figured out what, but we knew they were never quite the same. If chosen by the Great Lykos, they were never seen or heard from again.

You see, the whole town feared the Great Lykos, a giant man wolf. His wrath ensured the lack of prospering crops and the death of our livestock. He required a virgin bride of a certain age, which happened to be 12. His bride would bear him a child. During her pregnancy, our lands and livestock would be fertile. If she bore him a son—a lycan—we would have good luck for five years, and no sacrifice would be needed during that time. If she bore him a daughter, the child died instantly, her blood poured into the earth poisoning it, and we would be cursed. If she was barren, he would take two brides the following Beltane. In 1686, the bride was barren.

Macey was 12 the year the town priest came to visit. Macey was such a lovely child—all blonde hair and curls with blue eyes that could melt even the coldest heart in a glance. The priest had thirteen others, he told us, and it would not bode well with the Great Lykos. All of age and unmarried had to dance. She had to do the dance despite being betrothed, since she could not wed until the next full moon, two weeks after Beltane. There were 14 unmarried girls in the village of age to dance the maypole. Never before had we had that many. Twelve had been the highest number until now.

Tears filled Macey's eyes as she saw that we acquiesced, though our hearts trembled. As our last child, we were reluctant to give her up. If she were chosen, we would never see her again. How we felt about it, however, was moot. The rest of the town's safety depended on us to follow tradition.

So she danced. The music lifted their spirits, and the girls danced gaily about the pole. The rainbow of ribbons weaved in and out of the sunlight, while the flowers nodded in rhythm. The Great Lykos moved among the trees, always watching from a distance, until he had made his choice. In a blink, he was at the Maypole, more man than wolf; his long black hair disheveled, his silver eyes wide, and a great beard hung from his chin. His toothy smile was menacing as a robed arm reached out. He grabbed the purple ribbon to show his choice, and just as quickly, he grabbed the yellow ribbon lest the now frightened girls ran away before he got his second pick.

"You," he grunted to Macey, "You are my first, and will bear me a son. And you," he pointed to the other girl, her fist still attached to the yellow ribbon, "will be her handmaiden until such a time as I am ready for you."

Macey dropped the purple ribbon. "I will not. I am betrothed to another. I will not be your bride."

The people murmured amongst them as fear began to spread like a plague through the crowd. They moved away from the maypole as the Great Lykos wailed in anger, his eyes searching for her betrothed to make an example out of him. A shift of black flashed between the trees behind them.

"It is I, Father, who claim her for my own. Dare you go against me?" the lycan spoke from the edge of the woods. "It shall be your last breath." The wolf sprang, slicing his father's throat with such speed that none had seen him do it.

"It is with my last breath that I curse you all. I will take all of you to hell with me!" The Great Lykos' voice trembled, breathing a last hex against us all. The earth opened beneath him and devoured the 14 and his son along with him, and with that, his final curse, the annihilation of our town, began.

No babies were ever born to us again.

If you walk through the woods on May 1 of any given year, and it's quiet enough, you might hear the songs and laughter of 14 little girls emerge from the field. If the light is exactly right, you might even see them dancing in their ancient white dresses, flowers adorning their hair and dresses, holding bright colored ribbons attached to a wooden pole, erected in the dead center of the field. And if you are really lucky, you just might see the wolf and the girl dancing around the maypole.

When you wake up the next morning, you could find yourself in Hell.

THE CHAIR

Today makes five. My grandfather says five is a lucky number, but I'm not sure I believe him. The first four were nothing special, just your run-of the-mill state-mandated executions. In fact, the gurney in the room next door gets more business than I do, what with lethal injection considered "humane." I don't know about that either. Those who find their way onto my wooden seat and get strapped in generally seem remorseful. I don't know what pain they go through though I feel them quiver within the boundaries I provide. A rush of sticky heat overwhelms the air, and when it's finished—the last of their soul drifting into the ceiling—the metal cups from their heads always feel warm when they brush against my wood.

It's the memories that get me every time. I am privy to the last thoughts and delicate flashes of life revealed in those final moments. If I had lips to spill the secrets with, I'd swear to at least one man's innocence.

It was number three, and his name was Zion Jeffries. His wide girth crammed in between my seat and arms as he sat down. Listening to the walls chatter around me, I knew he'd committed a great crime against humanity. Convicted of the kidnapping, rape, and murder of three very young sisters and their mother, the attacks were especially brutal, earning him death by electrocution. The first to sit in my chair without a choice, he was also the first to be innocent.

As his last fleeting memories disappeared with his brain function, Zion had no recollection of his crime. There were short memories of his time spent in jail, time spent with his family, and the last day on his job as a car mechanic. A woman entered the shop with three tow-headed little girls following her.

"Excuse me?" she said. Zion looked her direction.

"How can I help you?" he said, his voice filled with

pleasantries.

"My car-" She looked down as heat colored her cheeks. "-it's broken down about a block away. Can you please help? Yours is the first shop I come to. I don't have any money."

Zion followed the woman and her girls down the block to where an old Buick sat, half on the road, half off. Smoke black as pitch escaped in billowy clouds from the creases of the rusty hood. He popped it open and leapt back as flames reached their long fingers out to embrace the oxygen.

"Run! If the fire reaches the gas, it will explode!" Zion cautioned the woman.

She pushed the girls ahead of her, and they ran back towards the shop. Zion followed, his curses airborne on the wind behind him. When they reached the shop, he left instructions for his assistant, grabbed the fire extinguisher from the wall, and took off towards the old Buick again.

"I'll be back shortly!" Zion shouted in passing. He paused at the door. "There's coffee and some bottled water in the fridge. If you need to call someone, there's a phone in my office."

Zion rushed back to the Buick, the nozzle on the extinguisher pointed and ready. The thick spray choked him, but he didn't stop until the last flame was out. He looked the smoking engine over, knowing it was too hot to do anything with. No, he'd have to tow it to the shop and look it over in the morning. He wiped the sweat from his brow with the rag he kept on him and headed for the shop. When he arrived, he found his assistant, the woman, the girls, and his personal truck gone. The note he left for his assistant glared at him from the counter, but nothing had been added to it. He swore. He'd wanted to touch base with the woman before she left. Now, he didn't even have her phone number. He called his assistant, but after getting the man's voicemail for the umpteenth time, he jumped in the company tow truck, hitched up the Buick, and towed it back to the garage.

The next morning, Zion awoke

to find his truck in his driveway, the tow truck gone, and the police swarming the property. As the cuffs clicked around his wrists, he took in the drawn faces of his family. All three of his boys openly wept. He could tell by the set of his wife's jaw she barely held it together. He saw his boys for the last time. His wife became a distant memory as well, as the evidence piled up against him. The tears shed now were his own.

Even then, on the chair, tears spilled behind the mask. For the first time the soul wasn't at rest, I was more than just a piece of wood formed into a chair, and the first time I felt what I could only describe as remorse. His tears left stains down to the very core of my creation.

With four came relief. Definitely guilty, the horror of his memories eliminated whatever remorse still remained.

Now, today makes five. I've heard five is a lucky number, but I'm not convinced. Three gave me heartache. Four gave me horror. What luck could five possibly bring?

I guess I'll know in a few

minutes.

TEARS OF A SINNER

"A rich man is always in need of a good wife," I read somewhere in an article about Jackson Bruning, the world's most eligible bachelor. The most intriguing part of the article, however, was the fact there were absolutely no pictures of the man anywhere to be found. In this technical day and age that was very rare, but, I suppose, could happen. I wasn't happy the only information I had on my betrothed was an article written by an untrusted source and had no pictures to swoon over.

My parents spent a great deal of time talking about him, his good fortune, and his generosity towards his fellow man. However, when I asked them about his appearance, they never gave any description other than tall, dark, and handsome. Perhaps they did this on purpose so I would dream my own daunting idea of what and who he was. I do know that by the time we officially met, I already loved him.

86

When the letter arrived inviting me, Clarice Fortune, to dinner, my heart lurched. Time passed as slow as time is wont to do when something special approaches, but finally, the night arrived. I donned my finest dress, borrowed a drop of the sweet perfume my mother wore, and dabbed a bit of rouge on my cheeks. Butterflies flitted through my chest. I hoped my appearance pleased him.

The threat of snow tingled my nostrils; I shivered as a cool evening breeze blew past me. I waited with trepidation at the esteemed La Chef Passionale, a place that required reservations made months in advance, to meet my mysterious fiancé. He was late. Of course, he was late! I waited another thirty minutes, and when he still didn't show I made my way out of the restaurant, tears falling one at a time. They splashed on the ground as I walked, following me like a breadcrumb trail.

A man approached me, his black top hat a sinister shadow over his handsome face. A teardrop tattoo rested just under his eye. I shivered, understanding what it meant. He stood in front of me, his dramatic black cape fanning out to block every attempt to go around him. I looked around in panic, trying to find someone who could help, but to my dismay, we were the only two on the street. It was as if everyone scattered when the clouds hid the moon, and this evil stepped out from the darkness.

"You are very beautiful," the man said in a surprisingly pleasant voice. A chill ran down my spine as his finger slid down my jawline. He pulled my hand to his lips and kissed it. "What are you doing out here on these streets alone this time of night?" He purred.

"I...I...I'm supposed to be meeting someone," I stammered, my terror so great my heart hammered against my chest. I shivered again and shrunk away from him. "He will be here any minute."

"Indeed, perhaps he is here right now." He stepped back suddenly and bowed in a grand gesture, his hat in one outstretched arm. "I am Jackson Bruning, and I apologize for being late. There was an emergency I had to attend to."

His tongue ran across his lips as he spoke. I shivered again. He was not at all what I'd expected.

"I have confirmed that our reservations are still available. Clarice, would you please join me?" He turned and offered me his arm.

I realized suddenly that as much as I didn't want to join him, I had to. I *had* to, for all the years spent pining away after him. I *had* to, for myself. I took his arm, and we walked back to the restaurant.

To my delight, he didn't look nearly as sinister in the soft light of the restaurant. He'd removed his top hat to reveal a head of thick and curly ebony hair. His blue eyes sparkled with life, and his teeth glistened beneath every smile, which happened often. Images of our future life together distracted me, intensified my feelings, even as my heart tried to warn me. Attentive through the multi-course dinner, I studied everything about him and memorized as much as I could. I never wanted to forget this moment. His was a life of adventure and excitement while mine composed of the very boring, run-of-the-mill life of a secretary. I feared he would find me dull.

"Why are you so mysterious, Jack?" I asked over dinner.

"I don't like people prying into my private life," he said over dessert. "Believe nothing you read about me. They have glamorized it all. I work hard for my fortune, but they don't want to tell you that." He rose from his chair and discarded his napkin to his plate. "Come, darling, let's carry our conversation somewhere more private."

My heart beat ferociously in my chest as I allowed him to seat me in his luxurious limousine. The car took off smoothly and before I knew it, we arrived at his house. Again my heart gave warning, which I ignored. Instead, I admired my future home and the fastidious nature with which he kept it.

"Does it meet your approval?"

Heat crested my face as I nodded and swallowed the lump in my throat. "It is beautiful. Any woman would be lucky to live here."

"Not just any woman, Clarice—*you*—and you will be here forever." He embraced me, and I let my guard down, just as hungry for his touch as he seemed to be for mine.

"Forever sounds like a long time," I whispered.

"You have no idea," he answered, his breath tickling my ear. He stepped back, and music streamed from the house. He cupped my hand in his, and we spun together in a dance foreign to me. He filled the rest of the night with hospitality and courtesy. He was the gentleman my parents claimed him to be, and by night's end, I'd fallen truly in love with the real man.

He paused in the foyer, knelt down on one knee, and reached for my hand. He slid a beautiful diamond ring onto my fourth finger. "Clarice Anastacia Garland, would you do me the honor of becoming my wife?"

A quiet fortnight later, I became a married woman. Emboldened by our bond, I decided to investigate that night.

"Darling, why do you have a tear tattooed on your face?" I asked him just before he bedded me.

He responded by awakening my body in places never woken before. As gentle as he was rough, he took his time to ensure my pleasure before gaining his, exploring my body into a pleasure I had never known. When we were spent, he tenderly tucked me into his embrace, and I rested my head on his shoulder. He kissed my neck, small splashes that tickled like a feather, to an urgent suckling that brought goosebumps to my flesh and aroused me once more. As a quiet moan left my lips, he bit, soft at first, then so hard he broke the skin. I gasped as the sting of pain interrupted my arousal. My blood leaked down my neck, and he pressed me closer, drinking deeply.

He laid me against the pillows gently. Stars danced the air in front of me and swam behind my eyelids. The room spun madly. The tethers binding my soul to my body filtered away in a milky mist. His tongue licked my neck. He whispered in my ear.

"You are not my first wife. I mourn her with a tear, just as I shall mourn you with one. I may have taken your human life, but I give you eternity in exchange."

He met my eyes with his. On his face a second teardrop glistened underneath the old one. It would be the last thing I would remember of my old life.

WHAT THE SIGN SAW

Her eyes soaked in the scene—the crumpled car, blood stained windshield, and horror filled eyes surrounding her.

"No!" Frankie cried as the ambulance rushed away. The EMTs pronounced him dead on sight, but she didn't believe it. She would never accept he was gone. Her stomach flipped as the smell of burning metal blew past her. Her chest numbed. She choked on her breath. The pain! Oh, the pain. Why couldn't life be more simple? She leaned over and let her stomach empty. She pressed her cold fingers into her forehead and hid her face in her hands. Her chest burned with tears that would not come.

"Oh my god! No!" She doubled over and rested her forehead against the pavement. Her teeth pressed together as she rose up, anguish and dirt staining her upturned face, scarlet from the neon light above her.

"WHY?"

Del stopped singing along abruptly when her ringtone interrupted the music. The Eagles "Hotel California" morphed into a Snow Patrol love song. The smiling face of her fiancé lit up the screen, and she grinned in response.

"Hi," she cooed.

"How's the drive?" Jude's excitement filtered through the speaker.

Del looked out the window. She recognized the street, even if she didn't recognize the motel. The sign looked old, almost reminded her of something she once saw in a horror movie years ago, but she shook it off.

"I'm here." An absence of cars made pulling into the parking space by the office easy. "Something's weird about this place." It crept up her spine like tickling fingers, but she couldn't quite say why.

Jude's laughter made the phone buzz in her ear and her heart caught. "Of course there is," he said. "I'm not there."

"That's true." She opened her car door. The stale rush of desert air filled her senses, and a cool breeze ruffled her blue black locks. She leaned sideways and stretched her thin frame. "Ugh, I wish I weren't, either. Why am I doing this again?"

"Because you're an old softie who made a ridiculous promise to a dying woman."

"Hmm. Right. A dying woman who happens to be in better health than I am right now! How is Frankie, anyway?"

Jude paused before answering. "As ornery as she was when you left."

"Haha. She's not giving you too much of a hard time, is she?"

"Nah." His voice grew faint then returned stronger. "She wants to talk to you."

"Oh…"

Frankie's shrill voice interrupted. "Cordelia." Heavy breathing filled Del's ear canal from the speaker. "Are you there yet?"

"Yes, I just got to the Chapel Hills Motel actually."

"And? Is it everything you imagined?"

Reddish-brown corrosion climbed up the pole that said "Motel" at the top. The sun had lowered in the sky far enough for the automatic lights to come on. At least, the T-E-L lit up. The peeling yellow paint revealed the long hours the motel spent under the hot sun. The guestroom doors had faded until the original color was no longer recognizable. The way someone had set the rickety, rusty metal chairs haphazardly along the surprisingly clean cement patio made her feel uneasy, as if this place were from a bygone era, and she trespassed. She couldn't tell Frankie that, however. She'd expect pictures, and Del, being a good daughter, would Photoshop every single one of them, erasing the telltale signs of age. She closed her eyes, hoping that fresh paint and shiny doors would replace the reality standing before her now. This would never do, but she couldn't tell Frankie that. She swallowed the lump of dread in her throat and returned to her conversation.

"Yeah, it is. In fact, it's more than I expected." She lied smoothly.

"Oh!" Frankie answered cheerfully. "Is it packed? It used to be so packed, we had to call a week in advance! Tell me, Cordelia, is it packed?"

"No, not packed. It's a Saturday, so I expect it will be soon." At least Del could be truthful about that. The sign reached the interstate, but besides a bar, there was little else nearby—no gas station, no convenience store—not unless you counted the lone pump to the left of the office and the tiny hotel room sized store on the right. O-P-E-N scrolled across the marquee, followed by advertisements for rooms, gas, liquor, and toilet paper.

"What room did they give you?" Excitement made the voice on the other end squeak. "Did you get seven? Did you ask for seven?"

"I haven't gotten that far yet. Why is it important?"

"It's the room I always stayed in, well, at least when I first started going there."

"Okay." Del ducked back into the driver's side door of her little alien-green Kia Soul and snatched her Coach bag from the passenger seat. The well-oiled office door opened easily, and Del stepped through it. She let a smile change her countenance as she approached the clean and orderly front desk where a small woman about 25 years old stood. Baby pink bubble gum cracked in her mouth as an index finger twirled a long, black, springy lock of hair. Her cleavage burst from the center of a red gingham button-down shirt. The finger released the hair, she sucked the gum back between her molars, and her straight, though large, white teeth showed in a big return smile.

"Howdy," the girl said. "What can I do you for?"

"I need a room, please," Del said. She looked at the tag on the girl's left breast. "Bunnie."

"Ask for number seven!" emitted from the cell phone. Heat crept across Del's face.

"Is number seven available?"

Another smack of gum preceded the snort Bunnie gave in response. "Sure thing." She pulled a clipboard out from underneath her desk and set it on the counter in front of Del. "Fill this out, and I need to see your I.D." Gum bubbled from her lips and popped softly.

Del shifted position and pressed her cell phone between her chin and shoulder. Her knees bent as she leaned in to begin writing. "Frankie, I have to go. I'm starting to get a lot of static, and I need to get checked in. I got Room 7. I'll call you when I'm settled in, okay?"

"The phones in the rooms don't work, Ms… Cordelia?" Bunnie glanced at the half-filled out paper. Humor lit up her sapphire eyes as they penetrated Del's lemon lime ones.

"It's Del, and that's okay. I have my cell phone." Del pushed the paper back towards Bunnie.

"Those don't work too good around here, either," Bunnie said. "You'll get a lot of static unless you're outside, and you're pretty much in a dead zone in the room. Cable's spotty too. You'll get HBO and a local station, a different one every day, and that's about it. Sundays you can pick up the local preacher on Channel Two between 11:00 AM and 2:00 PM." She checked Del's ID with the information on the paper and looked at Del again. "You still want the room? You can get cheaper rooms with full cable and full bars one exit further down the interstate." The last came out in a whisper with furtive glances cast around as if she expected someone to walk in on them.

"Thanks, but I still want the room." Del flashed a half-hearted smile as Bunnie moved to the register.

"You didn't say how many days? We got a special, stay three nights, get a fourth free. You want the special?"

Del counted her itinerary in her head. It shouldn't take her four days to do what she'd promised her mother six months ago, when Frankie stayed in the hospital battling lung cancer.

"Yeah, I'll take the special." *And hope I won't need it,* Del thought to herself.

A bubble snapped across Bunnie's lips, leaving a film of baby pink on them. "No refunds," she said, softly slurping the gum back into her mouth.

"I'll take my chances." Del said. Bunnie slid the key across the desk. "Thanks."

"Sure thing." Del started to turn. "Wait!" Bunnie shoved a business card in Del's face. "In case you need something, you don't got to come to the office. Sometimes you can get a bar or two on the porch."

Del took it without looking at it and shoved it in her purse. "Well, thanks. That's... thoughtful." *What kind of motel is this the phones don't even reach the office?* She turned to the door and looked through the glass. The L-shaped motel had no numbers on the doors, and they all looked the same. "Um, which one is number seven?"

Bunnie giggled. "There's only one seven," she said, her gum snapping cheerily. "It don't matter which way you start. Your key only fits one door."

Unease settled in Del's core. Frankie had praised this place, but she couldn't shake the trepidation she felt. "I suppose there's only one number one, too?"

"Well, yeah, duh," Bunnie smiled through the sticky haze on her lips. "Except it's over there." Her well-manicured index finger pointed to the door furthest from the office. "Seven's in the center..." she paused, snapped her gum again, and finished, "...dead center. Ain't no second guessing."

Del understood, but the explanation did nothing to quiet her bellyache. She pushed the door open in one swoop and the bell jangled loudly.

"Oh, I almost forgot." Bunnie said. The camaraderie had left her voice. "It's the second Saturday of the month."

The flat tone made Del turn. The light in Bunnie's eyes had dimmed. In fact, it seemed like the entire office had darkened slightly like a bulb had just blown out without blinking. "Yeah, it is. What happens on the second Saturday of the month?" One of Del's eyebrows arched neatly, sending half her forehead into double ripples just below her hairline.

"Oh," Bunnie's tone brightened too quickly, which only made Del more curious. "Nothing much, really. That bar across the street usually has a good band if you're looking. They have better bands on second Saturdays. Awful lot of carrying on, too, if you ask me. This place'll be full before morning. Call me ASAP if anyone bothers you."

That knot of unease doubled as Del exited the office. She stood by her car and counted the doors. Number seven from either end was indeed the same door, hosting the entire corner of the L.

"Well that's a nice break, at least," Del said aloud to no one. She moved her car to the closest corner spot, grabbed her suitcase, and pushed the key into the doorknob, only to meet resistance. The key wouldn't turn.

"You've got to be kidding me," she said, letting her breath escape in an audible sigh. She stepped to the door to the left, but the key didn't fit that one either. She repeated at the door on the right, only to meet the same result. In fact, each lock had its own unique shape. The key wouldn't even go into the other locks. She looked at her key a little closer and noticed that it had no teeth, only an open space shaped like a heart. Anger flashed through her. She wanted to stomp into the office and smack the gum right out of Bunnie's mouth. She inhaled, closed her eyes, and stuck the key in the door again. It resisted like before, but then she gave a little twist, and another. With a third twist, the door opened, and the stale air of a long vacant room hit her.

A layer of dust covered everything and swam in the sunlight that streamed from the mercury colored curtains covering the lone window. A dull sienna bedspread covered the creaseless bed. An electric alarm clock blinked a lime green reflection against the fake mahogany of the nightstand it occupied. The feeling of stepping back in time hit Del again. Even the small table and chairs set in the furthest corner of the room seemed dated. It made no sense to her, however, as the motel was in an ideal location just off the highway. It should have more business than this. She set her bag down and moved to the nightstand. She bent over and coughed, sending more dust through the air. She picked up the telephone handset and listened. Beep. Beep. Beep.

"Interesting," she said, as she remembered Bunnie's words. She pulled the clerk's business card out and looked at it. "No signal in the room, she said. I wonder…" She pulled her cell phone out. Four bars at the top indicated she had service. Her brow creased, and she scratched her head briefly before she grabbed a washcloth from the towel rack and dusted the room. She plugged in her phone to charge. She put the craziness out of her mind as she unpacked, resisting the urge to call Jude until she finished.

When she finished unpacking, she grabbed her cell phone, noting she only had half a bar this time. She grunted and walked towards the window, watching the bars as she went. This only gained her one full bar. She opened the door and stepped outside the room. Two more bars filled up and she smiled. "That'll do," she murmured as she swiped the seat of the closest chair and sat down.

"This place is bizarre," she spoke into the mouthpiece when Jude's smooth tenor answered the call.

"How so?"

"The desk girl… she said the phones in the rooms don't work, and that the motel was in a dead zone, then handed me a business card. Dust covered the room like no one had slept in it in years and there's not a soul here. I'd expect more business since it's just off the highway."

"It's only a small town, babe," Jude said, his voice taking on the tender tone he used with her whenever she seemed paranoid. She usually liked it, but sometimes, like now for instance, it rubbed her the wrong way.

"I'm not paranoid, Jude. I'm just saying it's weird. I mean, the motel is right off the interstate and the city is only ten minutes away. It's Saturday, and their rates are pretty fair considering what most cost. It's not the most updated place, but still.

I'd expected this place to be packed, that's all."

"Okay. You get unpacked okay? Made your dinner plans?"

"Yeah. I'm going to the bar across the street. Bunnie says-"

"Bunnie?"

"The desk girl, gum smacking bimbo and all. Anyway, she says the band will be extra good tonight. Supposedly it will be busy and so will the motel afterwards."

"Haha. Well, just don't fall in love with any of the rednecks you'll meet there."

Del chortled in response. "Trust me, Jude, you are all the redneck I can handle."

Another car pulled up to the office space. Bunnie stepped out of the office, a big pink bubble protruding from her lips. A big burly man with a tribal tattoo on his bald head, a flannel button down shirt with the sleeves ripped off, and tight jeans hugging his gigantic thighs stepped out of the car. He wrapped Bunnie in a tight embrace, pulled the gum from her mouth, cupped her butt cheeks in his big beefy hands, and kissed her deeply on the lips. Bunnie leaped and wrapped her legs around his waist, tucked her breasts in under his chin, and smothered his face with hers.

"Oh gross," Del said.

"What's gross?"

"PDA. Bunnie and some scary-looking guy are making out right here in the parking lot."

Laughter made the phone vibrate against her ear. "Since when do you have a problem with PDA? You're the first one to kiss me anywhere, and I can think of several make out sessions on the park bench!"

"This is just vulgar though. I mean he's got his hands all over her ass, and she's practically twerking on his hip! Oh gosh. Are they going to do it right there on top of the car?" She couldn't tear her eyes away as the man sat on the hood of his car and Bunnie spread out on top of his lap.

"Welcome to Hicksville, love!" Jude's laughter tickled her insides.

"You laugh, but he's got his hand up her shirt now, and not on her back either!" She breathed heavily into the phone. "I don't think she's wearing a bra."

"Hahaha! I'm jealous. Wish I had my own porn happening right in front of my eyes."

"Eww, Jude. Just… no. Ugh, now she's on her back on the hood and he's on top. There's thirteen available rooms here. Why can't they go in one?!"

"Hahahaha. I don't know. Maybe employees aren't allowed, or she has to keep an eye on the desk or something."

"Yeah, she's really keeping an eye on the desk alright. If I were a robber, I'd be home free for all the desk watching she's doing." When skin started to show, Del got up from the chair and went into the room. Static crackled loudly through the earpiece. "This sucks. If I stay outside, I have bars, but I'll see a lot more of either of them than I want to. All I get in the room though is a bunch of static. I think I'll just take a nap. Talk to you later, Jude." She waited for him to say goodbye before she put the phone back on charge. After closing the curtains tightly to avoid the graphic public affection taking place just beyond it, she fell on the bed. Before she knew it, she was fast asleep.

A different ringtone woke her from a deep sleep. Not Jude, but Frankie. The small white flash from her phone offered the only light in the room. Darkness overwhelmed the room so much she couldn't see her arm stretching to the nightstand until she picked up the phone. Frankie. She sighed and swiped the screen to answer the call.

"Hello?" She rubbed an eye with her free hand, sat up, and pressed her back against the headboard.

"Hi, darling!" Frankie gushed. She had one of those exhausting voices that always sounded excited over the phone.

"Hi."

Distress laced Frankie's voice now. "Am I disturbing you?"

"No. I just woke up, that's all. I'm glad you called."

"Oh! Good! I just wanted to check on you since you hadn't called me back yet! I got a little worried."

"I'm sorry. I got a little distracted and then fell asleep."

"Have… yumph buzz shoosh…" The phone crackled harshly, blocking Frankie's words.

"I have a really bad signal, Mom. Let me call you back, okay?" The static hurt Del's ear so she hung up without waiting for an answer. She flicked on her phone's flashlight and shined it around the room. Her arm stretched out far enough to switch on the small lamp on the nightstand, and she slid off the bed. An urgent need to pee led her towards the bathroom, but she stopped abruptly about a foot from the door. A vase filled with a dozen fresh red roses had been placed at the center of the table where there had been nothing before. Her eyes flicked to the motel room door. The chain still hung across the door and the deadbolt remained in the locked position. Cold fingers ran up her spine and icicles pricked her scalp. Her heart stabbed in her chest as she moved carefully towards the table. Someone had gently tucked a small card between buds. She hesitated a moment, but tentatively pulled it out with shaking fingers. A delicately drawn heart decorated the envelope. Del turned the envelope over. The same heart was stamped in red wax, sealing the envelope shut. She broke the seal carefully and pulled out the card. Duplicates of the envelope heart covered the front. Old fashioned penmanship greeted her from the opened card.

"To my dearest love," she read aloud, "Your beauty outshines these roses." She snorted loudly. "Cheesy but sweet. Now, why didn't Jude sign it, and how did they get in here?" She moved to the rotary phone and picked it up. It still had no dial tone, only the incessant beeping of a busy signal. "Ugh! This sucks!!" She opened her curtains and saw the same car sat in the office parking space. Del decided to visit the office.

"Hey, how's everything? Is the room okay?" Bunnie asked between pops of gum as Del walked towards the desk.

"Actually..." she paused. She hadn't thought through what she would say. "Um, I'm a little concerned about the security here. I locked up, fell asleep, and when I woke up, a vase of fresh roses sat on my table with a cheesy card. How could that be?"

"I don't know. Buck and I have been here all day and not a single car came through. Are you sure it wasn't just a dream?"

Yeah, I know exactly where your attention was, Del thought but held her tongue. "I'm pretty sure, considering it was my mom calling that woke me up," she said instead.

Bunnie held up her cellphone. The bars were empty. "That's impossible," her gum snapped. "There's no cell reception here."

"I get a couple bars out on the porch. Maybe it's your carrier." Del retorted. "How did the roses get in my locked room?"

"I don't know. I didn't see anyone or anything but you go in and out of that room. Why did you ask for that room anyway?" A couple cracks of gum broke up her sentences.

"My mom asked me to. She used to stay in it all the time."

Bunnie's eyes rolled up and her jaw chewed quickly. She met

Del's gaze again. "Hmmm. That's an interesting story. No one's rented that room in a while. We've had a lot of customers over the years, though. Can't say as I'd remember. Besides, I prob'ly wasn't even born yet." Another pop of her gum confirmed her youth. "You do look kinda familiar though. You sure you never been here before?"

"No. I live in another state and don't travel much." Del tapped the counter with her key absently. Nothing added up. She needed more time, however, and her stomach began reminding her it had been several hours since she'd eaten last. "Well, please pass on my thanks to whoever left the roses. They are gorgeous," she said as she left the office.

The bar across the street opened, and the music flowing from it seemed lively. She stuffed the keys in her pocket and crossed the street. The music, a cross between southern blues and country with a modern twist, increased in volume as she neared the bar. She stopped at the edge of the parking lot and looked around. The bright yellow and pastel colors gave a sharp contrast to the motel across the street. In fact, looking behind her, the motel became grayscale compared to the tropical hues of the building in front of her. Cars polka-dotted the parking lot. A large Stetson with a crab sitting on its crown lit up the center of the bar's facade, casting a yellowish hue on everything beneath it. "The Caribbean Cowboy" written in a rope text, lit up the space southeast of the Stetson. Del chuckled. All the dread filling the pit of her belly floated out with her laugh. Dancing lights splashed across the darkened windows and shadows of movement followed them. The building itself reminded her of a beach house. Lifted on stilts, the long ramp that ran down one side of the full deck reminded her of a place Frankie had told her about once. The significance of this knowledge escaped her at the moment, but she knew it held importance.

Wide steps led her to the entrance, where another crab-ridden Stetson greeted her. When she opened the glass door and stepped inside, the warmth of the place surrounded her. The band changed songs and played a unique cover of Magic Carpet Ride she liked. A young woman with raven black hair greeted Del and led her to a table near the band. She set a flip flop shaped menu on the table and went back to her station. Del picked up the small placard from the center of the table. "Under the Influence," she read. "Live Saturday night only! No cover charge!" She set it back down and poured over the menu until another raven haired woman, this one older, came and took her order. As the evening wore on, her shoulders softened, her breathing calmed, and she felt relaxed for the first time since she'd arrived here.

"Excuse me," a man said from beside her. She turned and looked into the deepest steel blue eyes she'd ever seen. The brown Stetson on his head covered most of the graying hair along his temple and defined his chiseled jaw. "May I have this dance?"

Del's eyes shot to the floor as her breath caught. His snakeskin boots came to a sharp point at his toes, and it surprised her to see silver spurs strapped to the heels. She followed his body with her eyes, though she didn't mean to, taking in the crisp look of his denim jeans, large silver belt buckle, plain white button-down shirt partially covered by a brown dress jacket the same shade as his hat. Before she knew it, she agreed to the dance.

"You look beautiful tonight," he said. His eyes roamed over her body appreciatively.

"Ha!" She scoffed. "I didn't even do anything special. I just came for dinner."

"It doesn't matter. You don't need anything special. You're beautiful exactly as you are." He stretched his arm out and spun her into his chest and back out again as the song ended.

"Thank you for the dance," Del said politely. She didn't understand how she could feel so elated and apprehensive at the same time. Disloyalty to Jude pinged her emotions as well. She tried to move around him, to return to her table, where her still steaming dinner waited. Her stomach grumbled in appreciation. The man stepped in front of her, blocking her escape.

"Don't you remember me?" He asked. Worry lines creased his forehead. Confusion speckled his eyes.

"No, I'm sorry. We've never met before." His hand lingered on her arm, but he let her pass. He followed her to her table and stood there silently for a moment before moving on. His departure left her alone to eat her tilapia in peace, and she temporarily forgot him. She wanted to call Jude, but found the bar too lively for conversation. She looked out through the windows as she waited. Unidentifiable shadows moved beyond the glass, catching her attention. She couldn't see who or what it was. She couldn't see anything beyond the window but an open field. The motel wasn't there. Her car was invisible. She rose, confusion marring her soft complexion.

"Can I get you anything else?" the waitress said as she dropped the check on the table. Del looked up at her, startled. She put her hand on the waitress's wrist.

"The motel across the street…" she paused, trying to figure out what to say.

"What about it?" The waitress stood there patiently.

"It was there when I came in, but I can't see it now." Del said. She fully expected the waitress to look at her like she was crazy, but she didn't.

"Yeah, I hear that a lot. That glass is not the best for seeing out of, especially at night. It tends to reflect the opposite side." She pointed to the glass on the other side of the bar. There, cloaked in shadow, stood the silhouette of the motel, the sign with its crimson glow appearing upside down on the ground.

"Wow!" Del said. Unease twisted in her belly again, threatening to expel the new contents within it. She swallowed hard. "That's really strange!"

"That's what everyone says. Listen, if you need a room tonight, you'd probably better get moving. The band will be done in an hour, and most of the drunks will be booking a room. It fills up fast." The waitress paused. "But, you knew that already, didn't you?"

Del nodded. "Bunnie warned me when I checked in earlier this afternoon. I wasn't sure I believed her."

"The band will be the worst. They always are." The waitress started to turn away but Del stopped her once more.

"Did you see the guy I danced with earlier?"

"No, I'm sorry. I didn't see you dancing with anyone."

Confusion clouded Del's eyes. "Big brown Stetson? Steel blue eyes?"

The corner of the waitress's lips moved down as she thought. She shook her head. "I've been working the tables, not paying attention to the bar. I'm sorry."

"It seemed like he comes in often." Del opened her purse and pulled out her wallet. She handed her credit card to the waitress along with the bill.

"I don't think so. I know most of the Saturday night crowd. Can't say as I've ever seen a guy in a big brown Stetson. Except the one in that picture over there." The waitress pointed to the wall behind Del. "You kinda look like the lady he's with, too. I'll be right back."

Del's eyes swept the bar. Stetson Man was nowhere to be seen. She walked over to the picture but didn't see the resemblance. When he didn't show up before the waitress brought her card back, she signed the receipt and left. The air was surprisingly cool and crisp, with an aromatic hint of sand and something else she couldn't quite place. The motel looked exactly the same, only now the "O" in the sign joined the T-E-L, leaving only the M unlit. She shivered and the unease entered her belly again. She really needed to hear Jude's voice. Five full bars at the top of her phone filled her with warmth as she dialed. Music floated from the earpiece, and she waited.

"Hey, you've reached Jude Devens. You know what to do at the beep." The beep sounded longer to Del than normal.

"I love you! Call me." The letdown overwhelmed her, and she stared at his face on her phone for a moment before dialing Frankie. She'd promised to call her back.

"Hi!" Frankie's enthusiasm should have boosted Del's spirits but it didn't. It was very odd how the doom and gloom had come over her so suddenly.

"Hi. I promised I'd call you back," Del tried her best to keep her emotions out of her voice. When Frankie responded with a sympathetic tone, she knew she'd been unsuccessful.

"What's wrong?"

"Nothing. Just tired. It was a long drive."

"You always did get homesick!" Frankie saw through her lie. "What's going on?"

"Nothing. The room is nice, the place is quiet still, but the bar across the road is pretty lively. I just came from there." Del paced the edge of the parking lot. She could hear the band playing faintly in the background. They'd moved on to a slow song she couldn't remember the name of.

"Anyone good playing tonight?"

"They're okay. Kind of a modern southern pop rock group trying to reinvent the classics. They did a nice cover of Magic Carpet Ride." She rounded the curb and drifted back the way she had come.

"I love that song! In fact, that's the first song I danced to when I stayed there. What a coincidence! What's the name of the band?"

"'Under the Influence'. They're singing some Travis Tritt song now. I think their set is almost over." She looked at the motel again. She noted that a few cars were parked in front of other rooms. Maybe she was being silly. Maybe her nerves were getting the best of her. After all, it wasn't every day she went out of state to visit a cemetery and stay in an old motel. "Mom?"

"They sound interesting." Frankie paused slightly. Del could hear her breathing hard. "What, dear?"

"What am I looking for again?" Del asked.

"The gravesite of Nelson P. Truitt. I need you to place a dozen red roses on it at exactly noon tomorrow."

Del groaned silently. Why did she agree to this, again? Frankie had never been forthcoming with anyone, let alone her. Maybe she could get real answers now. "And who is this Nelson Truitt? Why does it matter what time and how many roses I leave? I don't even know where I'd get roses to begin with."

"The city is only a few miles away, but if things are still the same, you should see an old man selling roses on the side of the road about 100 feet from the motel. He's there every day at the same time. At least, he was every time I went."

"When was the last time you were here?" Del stopped pacing and sat down on the curb.

"About fifteen years ago. I haven't stayed at the motel in many, many years though."

Fifteen years ago, Del felt invisible. No matter how hard she tried, Frankie seemed to look right through her. "So, what about this Nelson. Who is he?"

Frankie got quiet. Del could hear her struggling for breath. She had made a full recovery from the lung removal but still had bad days. Tonight sounded rough. "It's okay, Frankie. You can tell me later. Why don't you get some rest, and I'll call you tomorrow? My signal is getting weak anyway."

"Okay. Call me early. Bye."

Del hadn't completely lied. Her signal had weakened. Why had Frankie sounded relieved when she hung up? What was Frankie hiding? Dismissing it for now, she crossed the street and watched as the bars dropped one at a time. By the time she got to her door, the bars had all but disappeared. There would be no talking to Jude tonight.

A tap on her door startled Del. She wasn't expecting anyone. She rose from the bed and opened it. A middle aged woman stood there, her short chestnut hair framing her heart shaped face.

"Hi. I'm Madge. I'm at the desk. Just wanted to let you know there's a Leo DiCaprio marathon on HBO tonight." Madge hadn't looked at Del once since she opened the door. She watched the rooms along the bottom of the patio. "Oh, it's you! Welcome back."

"Excuse me?" Del said with amazement. She must have a double close by. It was the third time someone had recognized her, though she'd never been there before. "This is my first stay."

"We both know that's not true, but okay." Madge leaned in close and whispered conspiratorially. "Your secret is safe with me. I wouldn't want anyone to know it was me after last time, either." Madge pulled back and winked.

"No, I'm serious. I've never been here before. There was a man in the bar…"

"Yes, and you were pretty rude to him. Don't act like you don't know him."

Del's eyes widened to the point of pain. Stars crossed in front of them. "Because I don't? I've never seen him before in my life! How did you know, anyway?" She didn't care if her anger made her tone harsher than normal.

"You'll remember. You just need time. And I know everything." Madge sounded confident. The strangeness of everything confounded Del. She didn't know if she would make it through tomorrow if something didn't give.

"Time? No, I'm checking out in the morning." Del turned to close her door, but Madge whispered something behind her, causing her to turn around. "What did you say?"

Madge spoke louder. "I said, we'll see. You've never managed to check out on time. I've grown tired of it. Tomorrow I'm charging you if you aren't." Madge's patent leather Mary Janes clacked on the cement patio harshly as she stomped back towards the office. She turned at the last minute. "Mark my words. You'll change your mind!"

Del shut the door and stood with her back against it, breathing hard. Her whole body shook, and she started counting backwards.

"Please let there be bars, please let there be bars," she whispered in a half-prayer before she pulled out her phone. Two. "Thank you!" She dialed. Music filled the earpiece.

"One moment, while the party you are trying to reach is located." An automated voice said. More music filled the earpiece, and she bit her lip.

Jude's voice replaced the music. "Hey, you've reached Jude…"

She yelled in frustration. She resisted the urge to throw her phone. Her fists balled, and her eyelids squeezed together until tears spilled out. "Ugh! Where are you!" She screamed at the face staring up at her from the phone. The face she loved so much and needed right now. Banging on her door made her jump. She moved to the window to see who it was. Three of the band members stood on the patio, conversing and smoking. One of them hand-drummed on various doors. She realized they were drunk, high, or both. It would be a long night.

She sat on the bed and resignedly turned the television on.

Leo currently wooed Kate on the Titanic. Del blinked. This was her favorite movie. Perhaps things weren't as bad as she thought. This was no sinking ship, even though her stomach was still tied up in knots. She let her nervousness keep her aware. This was a very weird place, like no other place on earth, and it frightened her. This is the kind of place where someone would film a horror movie. She shivered and rubbed the goose bumps on her flesh away. Butterflies danced in her chest as they always did realizing she had that fairy tale kind of love with Jude that transcended time and space. She fell asleep feeling happy and loved, a stark contrast from the way she'd felt only an hour before. Jude filled her dreams—the first kiss outside the movie theater in falling snow, when she'd almost swallowed her engagement ring after he dropped in her wine, the way he played tag with the neighbor's kids—and she slept better than she had since she arrived.

Moonlight streamed from the gap in the curtains. Del sat up on the bed. A cold sweat covered her skin.

Her breath left a trail of steam in front of her. Her own icy digits left bumps on her arms. She had forgotten how cold the desert could get at night. She shivered and rubbed her arms with her hands. She turned the big box unit on and let the heat blast her. Movement in the corner caught her attention. She turned. Stetson Man stood there! One hand held a dozen fresh red roses. The other removed the old ones. Her eyes turned to her door. It was still locked from the inside. She gaped.

"What are you doing? How did you get in? Why are you here?" Her questions tumbled out as one.

Stetson Man stopped. He cocked his head as if he heard her, but he didn't answer. He glanced at the empty bed, tucked the old roses under his arm, and walked through the locked door. Del ran to the window, but he didn't appear on the other side.

Del screamed. She went on screaming for a long time, but nobody came. "Please," she begged the night. "What's happening to me? Help me. Please help me."

When she finally came back to herself, she tried to call Jude. She should have fled that horrible room, but her shaking legs made motion almost impossible. Finally, she staggered out to the rickety chair near her window.

"Hey, you've reached…"

"Ugh!" She almost threw her phone down, but realized it could be damaged if she did that, and she needed it. It was her only lifeline to the real world. Her ringtone blared, breaking the silence rudely. It was Frankie.

"Hi. Why are you up so early?" Del asked. It really was unusual for Frankie to be awake at 5:00 AM. Her evening slew of meds made her sleep deeply.

"I had a hard time sleeping last night. Too nervous I suppose."

"Nervous? About what?" She welcomed any distraction.

"As silly as it sounds, I'm really nervous about what you're doing today."

"Mom? Can I ask you a question?"

"What's that?" Frankie's breathing sounded heavy.

"Well, first of all, what are you doing?" A thousand things sprang to Del's mind, but none of them were anything Frankie would do. "What's the noise in the background?"

"I'm trying to sit up in bed. It's exhausting. I left the tv on." A half hearted chuckle ended the sentence.

"Oh." Sometimes Frankie had so much energy and life it became easy to forget that she'd been at death's door only a few months ago. "What I really wanted to ask is why is today so important to you?" Stetson Man hovered in the back of her mind like a sinister shadow.

A deep sigh filled the phone. *Uh-oh here it comes,* Del thought.

"You know I never really loved your father."

"I knew that." And she did. It had been drilled into her for as long as she could remember. "You never told me why."

"He's a good man, always has been. He just never..." Frankie stopped. Small, quiet weeping came through the phone. Frankie had put the phone down, but Del could still hear her. Another sigh came through the phone. Frankie had returned. "He just never ignited that spark I needed to feel. He never treated me wrong, never abused me, and never said anything unkind. He treated me like a queen. I do not ever regret marrying him, Cordelia. Not ever. But, Nelson... he held my heart. Maybe if I had loved your dad first, it would have been different. There just wasn't room after Nelson. Nelson took all of me with him when he died, and I never really got over it."

Del sniffed. This was not new, either. She'd always known her mom loved another man, but not who. It had impacted their entire lives together. Her dad worshiped Frankie, and Frankie didn't return it. Del could remember a time when she was ten, at the peak of her self-awareness, and her mother had been brushing her hair. She wasn't the blonde her mother was and had washed out green eyes. It always felt like that disappointed Frankie. Del struggled to feel beautiful and accepted, as every young woman did. Frankie's rejection hurt her more than she let on. Del handed Frankie the brush, and she'd stroke her hair, not ungently, but not tenderly either. They'd look in the mirror together and Del would see the hurt behind Frankie's brown eyes. Frankie always seemed haunted, even more so when she looked at Del.

"That's not news, either," Del said with more venom than she intended. Frankie gasped on the other end, and Del winced. "I'm sorry. I didn't mean that the way it came out."

"I deserve it though. I never fully appreciated what I had until it was gone. I mean that about you, too."

Del swung her leg, making a swishing motion, something she usually did when she became uncomfortable. This display of emotions on Frankie's part was unexpected. "You still haven't told me why Nelson is so special, why everything needs to happen with precision. There's so much going on, I-" Del paused, knowing what she wanted to say, but not able to get the words out. She never liked disappointing people. "I'm leaving in the morning. In fact," she said as she watched the sky begin to pink, "I'm leaving when we hang up. I can't take it here anymore."

"Del, please. I know you don't understand, but you will. I promise. Please don't leave. I'm…" Soft weeping drifted through the earpiece.

Del wanted to hang up, but she couldn't be rude. Her leg swung furiously beneath her, causing the whole chair to bounce.

"Del, I'm ready. Please, I need you to do this. It won't be much longer, I promise."

"I'll drop the roses off on my way out of town. That's the best I can do."

"I guess I'll have to be okay with that then. Thank you for doing this for me, Cordelia. I wish there was a way for you to fully understand what it means to me."

"Maybe if you told me why instead of getting upset, I might. So many peculiar things happening, I just want to come home."

"It's always been kind of crazy there. For such a small hole in the world, an awful lot happens. Nelson is my deepest love, and he left me way too early. All I can do now is honor our love as often as possible. I haven't been out there in a few years because I haven't been well enough to go. If you hadn't promised to go this year, I would've had to. It's our 35th anniversary."

Anniversary of what? Del wondered. As far as she knew, they never had a bonafide relationship. Frankie married Del's father shortly after Nelson died. There hadn't been time for anything long term, at least that's what Frankie led everyone to believe.

"What's that mean?"

Before Frankie could answer, the motel came to life. The sudden cacophony of the still drunk patrons overwhelmed her, and her signal weakened. "You'll have to explain it to me when I get home. I'm losing signal again. Bye."

She disconnected the call and went back into her room. Since her decision to leave, she'd felt calmer, more in control of her emotions. Seeing the fresh roses on the center of the table only jarred her for a moment. Something strange may be happening, but she wouldn't be here long enough to find out what. She began repacking. She sat on the bed and sighed. *Where was Jude that he couldn't answer his phone?* She wondered. That only happened for two reasons—he was at work or driving. It just didn't make sense because neither of those would keep him from answering for this long. She looked at her phone again, nothing. She squeezed her eyes shut, and next thing she knew, the sun was high in the sky and someone pummeled on her door.

When she opened it, Madge stood there with a smug look on her face. "I thought you were checking out today?"

"I am. It's not check out time yet." Del looked at her empty hand. She turned to look in the room and saw her phone on the bed. The clock on the nightstand glared 11:25 AM. She blinked. "Oh."

"I told you! You never check out on time!" Madge scanned the room with her eyes. They rested on the open, packed suitcase. "I'm charging for today. You're over an hour late."

I thought checkout was at 11? Why is she lying to me? "I got the special! I woke up at dawn and must have fallen asleep. Dammit! I've gotta go!"

She wouldn't even have time to shower or finish packing. Del tossed a clean shirt on and ran a brush quickly through her shoulder-length hair before securing it in a ponytail. The time on the clock now read 11:45 AM so she grabbed the roses on the table and left everything else in the room. Buck's car wasn't in the lot anymore. Bunnie had left. Her fists clenched at her sides. Without a map, directions to the cemetery were desperately needed, but she'd be damned if she asked Madge. The dead zone meant navigation would be iffy as well. She hoped someone at the gas station she'd seen knew, since The Caribbean Cowboy didn't appear to be open. That seemed odd to Del somehow, too, as early rising drunks would be good breakfast business. She even drove into the parking lot to check. The closed sign swung gently against the door. Bodies moved around inside the bar, but she didn't have time to wait. Del promised to be on time, and noon approached too quickly. The bars on her cellphone signal lit up, and she managed to get the directions to the cemetery locked in before she lost connection.

The Eagles' "Desperado" filtered from the radio. She cranked the song, letting the lyrics calm her as they always did. With her windows down and dust flying behind her, she sang along as she saw the cemetery entrance. She turned in and nerves and dry heat choked her. Unable to sing anymore, the motor ran until the song finished.

Tap. Tap. Del didn't realize she'd closed her eyes until she opened them to the tapping. A man dressed in all khaki stood there, his name plate sparking in the sunlight. She cracked her window.

"Can I help you, Miss?" He bent down to press his face near her window. The lines on his face betrayed his age, despite the lack of silver in his hair

"I'm just here to visit a grave," Del answered. "My mother sent me," slipped through her lips before she could stop them, as if she needed an explanation for her trespassing.

The guard looked her car over, noting her out of state plates. "This is private property, ma'am. Perhaps you could tell me who it is you want to visit?"

"Um..." She had to think for a minute as the name escaped her. "Nelson P. Truitt, please. I believe he died 35 years ago today?"

The guard didn't answer right away. He scratched his hairless chin instead. Clarity struck his face moments before he responded. "Oh! Old Nelson! Funny you mention that name. No one has asked after him in several years."

She held up the roses. "My mother says it's their 35th anniversary, and I need to place these roses on his grave in exactly four minutes. Could you please point me in the right direction?"

"Oh, oh...uh...sure." He pointed to the small paved path straight ahead. "Take the 3rd path to the right, all the way to the end. His crypt is the last one in the row."

Del swallowed hard. *His crypt?* Frankie didn't mention a crypt. This situation just got bizarre, and the lump in her gut returned. The guard nodded solemnly, and she wondered briefly if that was just his nature or if he knew something she'd be better off knowing, too. He didn't say anymore, however, just turned away and walked back towards the small guardhouse she noticed for the first time. His exit was as curious as everything else around her.

"A crypt. Lovely." She muttered to herself as she pulled off slowly down the narrow path. "Dear God, Frankie! What have you gotten me into?" This came a bit louder as the path narrowed slightly and turned sharply. The crypt appeared a short distance ahead. Tall and wide, grey stone turned black on some corners, moss taking up residence on the others, it looked as menacing as it felt.

She put her car in park, grabbed the roses, and got out. Four stone steps led to four stone pillars. Rather than hosting a family name, as most crypts did, it only bore a single name: Nelson Preston Truitt. The engraving looked older than 35 years, however, and she wondered how long the crypt had stood before Nelson's remains entered it. Tiny fingers of ice crawled up her back, and she shivered. A small stone urn sat at the top of the steps in front of a pillar, and Del sighed with relief. She pulled the brown, decayed stems from the urn and replaced them with the fresh roses she'd brought with her. It didn't feel right to leave without saying anything, yet Del didn't know what to say.

"From Frankie," she said before resting her palm against the cold step. A shadow caught the corner of her eye, and Stetson Man lumbered around from the right side of the crypt.

"Hello, again." He tipped his hat in salutation. His steel blue eyes sparkled inhumanly in the sunlight. This did nothing to dull his appeal, only caused Del to become more intrigued.

"Hi," she answered. "What brings you here?"

"To meet you, of course." His voice held a confident nonchalance. What he was confident about, however, still remained a mystery.

"How did you know I would be coming here?" She stood up from the urn and backed away from the crypt. As handsome as he was, after the earlier visual, his being there completely creeped her out

His grin reached his ears. "You always come here." He stepped forward with his arms extended. Del stepped further away. "Gosh, I love it when you play coy."

"I'm...I'm...I'm..." her tongue grasped for words that refused to be said. She backed towards her car, afraid to turn away. "I'm not playing anything. I don't know who you are, and, honestly, you're beginning to weird me out." She flashed her left hand. "I'm engaged to get married to someone far from here."

Stetson Man laughed. "You always were. I'll become a distant memory when you go back to where you came from. Please, let me have this moment as a memory." He bowed low, and a country song drifted from a radio somewhere. He held his arms out. "May I have the pleasure of this dance?"

A cloud of dust kicked up behind them, and the smell of rubber burning on asphalt greeted their nostrils.

"What in the world?" Del turned towards the sound. A sapphire blue Dodge Charger with white pin-striping flew towards her. If she didn't know better, she'd think it was Jude, but he was a whole state away. Why would Jude be here?

Stetson Man danced into her view, bowed with his hand extended, and repeated, "My beautiful darling, may I have this dance?"

The song sounded familiar yet its lyrics and name skirted around her brain. Another screeching of brakes and more burning rubber distracted Del. She looked at the Charger again, this time searching for a look at the driver. Her heart leaped when she saw a flash of his dark goatee and tanned, tattooed knuckles curled around the steering wheel. More amazingly, Frankie occupied the passenger seat, though she seemed small for some reason. Jude came within inches of hitting Del's parked car head on, but managed to stop in time. Jude jumped from the car, grabbed Del, and gave her a long, hard, deep kiss right there in front of the crypt. Jeb applauded, breaking their embrace. Stetson Man stepped forward again, his arms still extended, and looked Del in the eye.

"I'll dance with nobody but you," he said, a stray sunbeam catching his eye and making it twinkle horrifically. He came close enough to grab for her. She moved closer into Jude's arms.

"Sorry, this dance is mine," Jude said, putting himself between Del and Stetson Man, his hackles raised and ready to fight. Frankie stepped out of the car, tears streaming from her eyes. She didn't cross the distance to the crypt. Instead, she stayed close to the Charger, trembling with her whole body.

"Nelson?" Frankie stage-whispered.

Del's chin fell to the ground. "This is Nelson?" she asked. *Of course it's Nelson.*

Frankie looked Stetson Man over before answering. "I'm not sure, honestly. He certainly looks like Nelson, but..." Her eyes shifted back to Del's after scanning the crypt. "But, how can that be? He died 35 years ago today!" She pointed to the broken M-O-T-E-L sign in the distant sky beyond the crypt. "The sign saw it all!"

"The sign?" Del said. The unease she'd been feeling all along turned to broken glass in her gut. Something was definitely wrong. Her brows buried themselves in her eyelashes.

"What about the sign!" She demanded.

The music shut off as abruptly as it started. The time for dancing had passed.

"The sign watched Nelson die." Frankie said somberly.

Stetson Man stared at Frankie hard then did the same thing to Del.

Del shivered when she felt his steely eyes soaking in every inch of her.

"Impossible. You don't look anything like Francesca." His tone accused Frankie of lying.

Tears streamed down Frankie's face again. "Impossible? You are dead, Nelson."

Nelson patted himself all over. "I don't feel dead. In fact, I've never felt so alive!" He extended his arm out to Del again and music played once more. "Dance with me!"

Del felt a pull on her body she found hard to resist. Nelson shimmered in the sun, and Frankie saw it.

"No! Don't! You can't take her! It's me you need to dance with!" Frankie moved towards Nelson's outstretched arms, but he disappeared behind the crypt before she could. Del felt completely stunned.

"I've had enough. This is complete nonsense. Let's go!" Jude said, pulling Del with him.

"What just happened?" Del's confusion dropped away. The reality of their arrival finally sunk in. "Why are you here?"

"I realized I couldn't let you do this..." Frankie responded.

"Let's go." Jude insisted. Del started toward her Soul, but he stopped her.

"Stay with me," he said, as he tightened her in his embrace. Del pulled Frankie into the Charger despite the insistence to stay. Jude flew out of the cemetery and onto the main thoroughfare. Del's cellphone lit up suddenly as a volley of texts came pouring in. They were all from Jude, all repetitive attempts from him to tell her they were on their way. Tears pooled on her eyelids and spilled down her cheeks.

"What's wrong, love?" Jude's concern colored his face.

Del's fist curled into a ball at the top of her belly. "It hurts, here, and I can't get it to go away." She lifted her cellphone. The tears she'd managed to hold back the whole time she'd been there suddenly crested and rolled over the edges of her eyelids. "I didn't know why you wouldn't answer. I got so scared and

I still am! Something bad is going to happen. I don't know why, I don't know what, and I'm powerless to stop it, and I know it's really going to hurt."

Jude reached over and pulled her closer. "Nothing's going to happen. I won't let it. Don't you know, the good, living guys always win?"

"I'm not so sure. I mean, this is supposed to be real life, not some horror flick! How did Frankie convince you to bring her here and why did she change her mind?" She turned to look Frankie in the eyes.

"She got something in the mail, then made me pack. We left within an hour. She didn't tell me much, only something about Nelson's ghost wandering and searching for his soul mate. She barely let me stop for anything but gas on the way, either. You know I don't answer the phone when I'm driving, so she did all the talking. She didn't want to freak you out, so she didn't say anything. When I realized she wouldn't tell you we were on our way, I sent texts every chance I could. I'm so sorry you just got them. Honestly, I thought you would hear my engine in the background."

Del looked back at Frankie through slitted eyes. "I did once. Frankie said it was snow on her tv."

The motel sign loomed ominously as they approached. Del wished she'd never checked in, and more importantly, never asked for Room 7. She should never have promised Frankie she'd do this. She shivered. So much mystery surrounding her. One person held the answers and Del couldn't remain silent any longer.

"What the hell is going on, Frankie? Why would you send me all the way out here if you could make the frigging trip by yourself? Do you have any idea the hell I've been through since I arrived?"

"I'm sorry, Cordelia. When you made that promise, I was too weak to argue. I never thought you'd actually follow through with it."

"Then why did you let me leave? Did you know what would happen?" Del tried to get Frankie to look at her and succeeded once, but the eye contact only lasted for a second.

"I didn't see the harm in it, honestly. I thought it might be nice for you to see a part of my past. If the postcard hadn't arrived, I wouldn't have forced Jude to come. Once I saw that card, though, I knew I had to intervene. My love life was a charade, but yours doesn't have to be."

"Poor dad." Del's nostrils curled.

Frankie pleaded with her eyes. "I tried to do right by your father, Del, I did. I can't help it my heart belonged elsewhere."

"I don't get it. Why is everyone here mistaking me for someone else? I've never been here. Roses showed up in my room despite a locked door, and then Nelson showed up and left a fresh batch then disappeared like a ghost through my door. Madge accused me of never checking out on time! What the hell is going on?"

Frankie pulled the postcard out of her purse. She gave it to Del. A picturesque scene of Del and Jude sitting on a park bench glossed one side. On the other side someone had scrawled "Can't wait to see you, my darling" without a signature or a name.

"Wait. Why is the front picture of me? This is from Nelson? Nelson doesn't know me."

"You kept saying on the phone how unusual everything was. You told Jude you'd stepped back in time. Nelson looks exactly the same as he did 35 years ago. He thinks you're me. That's why I made Jude rush down here. He's looking for me, not you. I'm his soul mate. I had to protect you." She laid her hand on Del's arm. "It's my fault he died."

Del and Jude just blinked at the revelation, numb from her revelation.

"I did it. I watched him die, because I knew I couldn't live without him, but I had to marry your father. I was already pregnant with you, he just didn't know it yet. Your father and I? We were only supposed to be a one night deal."

Del gasped. This surprised her. She'd always believed Frankie had met her father after her true love died, not the other way around.

"Yes, I have many secrets." Frankie reached a hand out and ran her index finger down Del's jawline. "You look like me, Cordelia. I won't let Nelson take you. I won't."

"Why did you insist that I stay in Room 7?"

The temperature dropped in the car suddenly. Del shivered.

"It was always only Nelson's room. He practically lived at the motel, had a lot of money invested in it. When he died, the motel proprietor said he was never renting that room out again. It would be kept as a memorial to Nelson instead. They never let me stay in it again. It was more curiosity than anything else. When I heard ownership changed hands, I decided I'd try again. I never considered it could be haunted. The memory of what I did has possessed me all these years. It kept me from being the person you and your father deserved. I'm sorry for that, Del. So incredibly sorry." She reached out and stroked Del's face again, a loving gesture foreign to Del.

Del turned her head sideways and looked at her mother from the corners of her eyes. Her brows scrunched together. Fear rose from her bowels and settled in her heart.

Jude saw the shadows settle on his fiancé's face. "Look, I don't give one fuck what's going on here. Whatever is going on in this backwoods ghost town is none of our business. I'm taking Del to the motel to get her stuff, and we are *all* leaving. If you hurry up, we can get out of here before dark even."

"No, I'm sorry. I have to stay. Just leave my suitcase in Room 7. I'll take over Del's reservation."

"No. I don't care about your past or your reasons." Del whispered. "You're coming home with us and that's final."

"No, it's not. I'm sorry, Del. I'm ready. I knew one day it would come to this. You are not meant for this." Frankie's pressed lips showed Del she meant it.

Jude didn't bother to slow down as they approached the motel. As he drove into the small parking lot, a ghostly figure wearing a big brown Stetson stepped out of Room 7 and directly into his path. Jude slammed on the brakes. The car skidded sideways and slammed headfirst into the motel sign pole. The force of the impact caused the motor to crumple into the dashboard. Del's body hit the passenger door, forcing it open, and fell out. Someone screamed close by. Jude's head hung at an odd angle against the back of the seat and a splash of blood decorated the windshield. Frankie's body lay sprawled against the trunk of the car, a pool of blood thickening beneath it.

Motel patrons stood in every doorway, gawking at the scene. Madge came running out of the office, yelling. "Oh my God! Not again!"

Del heard someone sobbing now, and Bunnie raced to her side. She pulled Del's head onto her lap. "Oh, honey! Is that your man?" Bunnie pointed towards the Charger, where Jude still remained in the driver's seat. Sirens wailed in the distance.

"Yes," Del wailed, "and my mother, too."

Jude's eyes opened, and he whimpered. Del willed herself to move at the same moment he staggered from the car. Blood poured from a gash on his head, but he focused on Del. He gripped her in an embrace so rough, she screamed in pain. Unable to hold each other up, they both collapsed to the asphalt and watched as Nelson reached into the back seat and grabbed Frankie's hand. Frankie accepted it, and he pulled her from the wreck tenderly. When she was free of the car, she kissed Nelson deeply, sealing her soul to his. They seemed to hover over the ground as they moved to Room 7. Tears slid down Del's cheeks as Frankie followed Nelson through the door.

"It wasn't real." Del said, relieved laughter bubbling from deep within her.

Jude hugged her tight. "It was real alright, babe." He kissed her with bloody lips.

"I'm never letting you go," she whispered into his ear.

He kissed her again. "Nope, never gonna happen."

THE THIRTEENTH YEAR

Only one mirror hangs in my house. It is positioned at the perfect center of our single-story home, covering the pantry door in the small kitchen. You can see the markings of where mirrors used to hang, but they were all gone now save that one. Despite my age, I remain in my home as the guardian of the mirror. Many have tried to gain access to it, but I, along with my two gargoyle companions, have eliminated them. I have been allowed to stand guard because my reflection no longer appears in the mirror. It has not for a very long time.

I believe I was eight the year Mr. Worthington moved in. Father had gone off to war, and Momma had to rent out a room in our house to make ends meet. She placed an ad in the small county newspaper, and Mr. Worthington answered. He rang the doorbell, and when I opened the door, my jaw gaped. He looked like he had just stepped off the page of a men's fashion magazine. His black hair glistened to his shoulders. A white band decorated his black top hat. Round wire-rimmed glasses perched on his narrow nose. The blackness of the frames perfectly set off the intensity of his ice-blue eyes. A thin black mustache hovered over his full lips. He held a black cane in his right hand, the lace spilling out from under his jacket sleeve playing hide and go seek with a silver parrot head clutched within his palm. His ebony jacket layered over a scarlet vest, and an ivory tuxedo shirt tucked neatly into onyx pants. A pair of slick black leather shoes completed the look. A tattered charcoal suitcase sat on the porch next to his legs.

"Hello," he said, revealing his perfectly white teeth. "Is your mother home? I have a meeting with her this morning."

Momma came down the hallway wiping her hands on a dish towel. She extended her hand in greeting. "Mr. Worthington? It's a pleasure to meet you. I am Amelie Pruitt and this is my daughter, Hanna. Please, won't you come in?"

Within the hour, Mr.

Worthington had given Momma a paper bag full of cash and stashed his suitcase in the guest bedroom. Just like that we had our first boarder. Little did I know he would be our only one.

Mr. Worthington helped Momma around the house. He fixed things that broke and tightened screws that came loose, just as Father would if he was home. He seemed a nice enough person, even if in all the years he lived with us I never did see him eat or drink anything. His refusal to join us at mealtimes bothered Momma, but she never let on. He never worked, yet his rent was always on time. I know that bothered Momma, too, but she never said anything. His money saved our home, and that's why Momma never questioned, and never told him to leave.

Not even when Father returned broken in body and spirit from the war. We needed Mr. Worthington and his money more than ever then. Father spent his days in a wheelchair scolding everything Momma did. She said it was because he was miserable, because he had a bullet lodged in his spine, but I didn't believe her. I think it was because Mr. Worthington was always there, and as such, they never had any privacy. I never saw Father and Momma kiss or hold hands anymore. Father's words were always sharp, even with me, and Momma stopped smiling. A darkness settled over our house.

The first mirror to go was Momma's. Father had thrown a glass at it one morning in anger and shattered it. Momma had cuts all over her arms and face from the falling glass. When Father did not apologize, Mr. Worthington tended to Momma's wounds and cleaned up the glass. Father hurled another glass at Mr. Worthington, breaking the second mirror, a large mirror hanging over the Queen Anne sofa in the foyer. He instructed Mr. Worthington to leave, who ignored Father, and cleaned up the broken glass before retreating to his room in silence.

One by one, the mirrors disappeared after that. I do not know who removed them, only the why. The glass had left Momma's face scarred, and she couldn't bear to look at herself anymore. To cover them was too great a temptation to torture herself, so they were removed. For several years, no mirrors hung on the walls of the house. Not one. Momma aged more rapidly than she should have, but Mr. Worthington—he remained as youthful looking as he did that day standing all dapper on our front porch. I have no clue how he did it. I only knew he could sell time if he desired.

When I was twelve, I came home from school one day to find Momma laying casually on the brown sofa in the living room. The disarray of the house revealed that something untoward had happened. Tears hovered on the edges of Momma's eyelids, one of which had traces of purple and black outlining it. Father's wheelchair sat empty in the hallway.

"Where's Father?"

Momma only blinked at me. I shook her gently.

"Momma! Where's Father?"

She blinked again. Her hands frenzied in her lap. She dropped her head to her chest.

"He's gone. He's been taken away." She mumbled barely loud enough for me to hear her.

"Where has he been taken?" Shock stained my voice.

"The army..." Momma swallowed hard. "They took him away." She looked at me sternly, all trace of tears vanishing quickly. "He's not coming back."

I saw pleading in her eyes. She wanted me to understand.

"Ever."

I touched her bruised eye, and she winced. I nodded my head and let her embrace me.

"I'm sorry, Hanna," she whispered.

Momma lost all her sunshine after that, and Mr. Worthington took care of her during the day while I was at school. He promised me that Momma would recover soon and once more be the Momma I needed. Every day I looked for changes, but it was my thirteenth birthday before I saw any.

I came home from school that day expecting the same as I had for the past year. I walked in the house and the sweet smell of rising dough surrounded me. Momma was baking! I didn't realize how much I missed her baking until that moment. I ran into the kitchen. She'd gotten dressed that morning. She'd even done her hair. She looked different, radiant. She looked like Momma, only a younger version of herself. She wore no makeup. She didn't need any. The sunny smile she wore gave her skin a shine I had not seen since Father went to war. I felt hope cresting in my chest. Maybe we could live normally again!

Momma's smile never left her face the entire day. She cooked my favorite meal, invited a couple of my best friends and their mothers over, and we feasted on coconut cake, my favorite. Just before bedtime, Momma made me stand in front of the pantry door. A cloth covered the door, and I grew excited. It had been many years since I had received something on my birthday. We never had the extra money. To my chagrin, Mr. Worthington joined us. He smiled at me, but my stomach churned. I believe it was that moment I knew there was something very wrong happening. I shushed my stomach, choosing to ignore the warning. I wanted this gift, whatever it was.

"Happy birthday, Hanna. Thirteen is such a special age. Though your mother resisted, I got you a little gift." Mr. Worthington's fingers clutched the cloth and slid it upwards slowly, revealing a mirror underneath. I gasped. Gargoyles imprisoned in gold bordered the full-length glass. The glass itself seemed translucent, beautiful. It made me look pretty instead of plain. I searched for Momma in the mirror, curious to see how she looked in it, but she did not appear. I searched for Mr. Worthington, but he did not appear either. Trouble grumbled from the pit of my belly.

"The mirror is magical, Hanna. Do not be afraid. It will only show you what you wish to see. You wish to see yourself beautiful, you will be beautiful. It will not show you anyone else, only yourself. Do not be troubled. It is a gift. Cherish it. Guard it, for others will want to take it from you."

His words confused me. "Why would someone want to steal a mirror?"

"Because it is valuable."

"Why can't I see Momma in it?"

"Because she does not wish to be seen," he said simply, dismissively. Momma smiled when I looked at her. I accepted his answer and let it go.

Today, on my eightieth birthday, I stand before the mirror. I see no reflection in it, not even the counters of the kitchen behind me. The gargoyles, no longer imprisoned in the gold border, are on either side of me. They came out on my twenty-first birthday, when I lost my reflection, and remained with me ever since. I assume they will remain with me as long as I own the mirror. There's a knock at the door. As they slide back into the gold border and I bring the cloth down, I catch a shimmer in the mirror. My time has been sold. The clock has run out. I know who is at the door.

He stands there dapper and demure. He tips his black top hat at me in greeting. He looks exactly the same as he did the first time I met him so many years ago.

People always said never to invite a vampire into your house. Too bad Momma never listened to other people.

ACKNOWLEDGMENTS

Without the dedication of my alpha readers, Paul Davis and Eric Keizer, this collection would still be a first draft. Without the support of my best friend and writing partner, Amanda Mabry, this collection never would have come to fruition. Without the wonderful writing challenges of Indie Ink, Write on Edge, and the Master Class writing prompt, these stories would not exist.

Most of all, without you, my dear readers, these stories could not come to life. Thank you for your love and support through reading and reviewing my work and enjoying it anyway.

The 13

ABOUT THE AUTHOR

Stephanie Ayers writes speculative fiction, where horror and fantasy collide. She is a self-proclaimed word whisperer and unicorn living in Ohio disguised as a human. She mothers her children and avoids all things housework and zombies. When she isn't doing any of these things, she can be found browsing thrift stores and flea markets with her husband, attending football games with her son, or binging on TV shows.

Stephanie has been a regular contributor and leader for Bloggy Moms and Just Be Enough, and currently writes content for Verblio. She is a strong supporter of the indie author community. She achieved Amazon best seller status in 2017 with the poetry anthology, Ambrosia.

Her debut novella, Til Death Do Us Part, was published by Bannerwing Books in 2013, and her work appears in several anthologies and collections, notably Absolution, Flash Fiction Addiction, and

Monsters: A TPQ Anthology. She currently has two serials to her name, the stand alone horror volumes of The 13 series and her new epic fantasy, the Destiny Defined series, which debuted March 7, 2019.

Her favorite quote is: "The blank page is a canvas on which the writer paints a story."-Stephanie Ayers

Subscribe to her newsletter here: https://subscribepage.com/o6e0l9

MORE BOOKS BY THIS

AUTHOR

Til Death Do Us Part
If the Shoe Fits

The 13 Series:
Tales of Illusory
Tales of Macabre

The Destiny Defined Series:
Wings
Elven Games

Anthologies:
Flash Fiction Addiction
Absolution: A Crazy Ink Anthology
Ambrosia: A Poetry Anthology
Tales from Our Write Side
Monsters: A TPQ Anthology
Endless Darkness

Precipice 2
Flash Fiction 1x50x100

Follow this author on Amazon and Bookbub to stay up to date on her releases.

Subscribe to her monthly newsletter and become a part of The Unicorn Herd.

Follow her on Facebook, Twitter, and Instagram. She is @theauthorSAM everywhere.

Did you enjoy this book? I'd love to hear all about it. I welcome reviews from our readers. After all, it is the best gift you can give an author.